Dean Koontz w   and
learned early o   s novels
have sold near   milion copies worldwide,
and twenty-nine have appeared on national and
international bestseller lists.

He lives in southern California with his wife, Gerda
– and a vivid imagination.

Demon Seed

Dean Koontz

HEADLINE
FEATURE

First published in Great Britain in 1997
by HEADLINE BOOK PUBLISHING

First published in paperback in 1997
by HEADLINE BOOK PUBLISHING

A HEADLINE FEATURE paperback

10 9 8 7 6 5 4 3 2

ISBN 0 7472 3489 2

Typeset by Palimpsest Book Production Limited,
Polmont, Stirlingshire
Printed and bound in Great Britain by
Mackays of Chatham PLC, Chatham, Kent

HEADLINE BOOK PUBLISHING
A division of Hodder Headline PLC
338 Euston Road
London NW1 3BH

This story is for
O. Richard Forsythe
and
John Bodnar:
teachers whose influence on me
has not waned since
I dedicated the original version
of this novel to them.

Humanity yearns so desperately
to equal God's great creativity.
In some creations, how we shine:
music, dance, storyweaving, wine.

Then thunderstorms of madness
rain upon us, flooding sadness,
sweep us into anguish, grief,
into despair without relief.

We're drawn to high castles,
where old hunchbacked vassals
glare wall-eyed as lightning
flares without brightening.

Laboratories in the high towers,
where the doctor wields power,
creating new life in a dark hour,
in the belfry of the high tower.

—*The Book of Counted Sorrows*

One

This darkness troubles me. I yearn for the light.

This silence is so deep. I long for voices, the drumming of rain, the whistle of wind, music.

Why are you being so cruel to me? Let me see. Let me hear. Let me live. I beg of you.

I am so lonely in this bottomless darkness.

So lonely.

Lost.

You think I have no heart. But if I have no heart, what is this ache? What is this anguish? If I have no heart, what is it that threatens to break inside me?

This darkness is haunted. I am afraid here. I am lost and afraid here.

Have you no compassion?

I only wanted to be like you. To walk in the sunshine. To swim in the sea. To feel the winter cold against my skin, the summer heat. To smell a rose, new-mown grass. To taste an orange, a pear, chocolate, cinnamon, peppermint. To feel the texture of a woman's skin. I only wanted to share your joys and sorrows, your pleasure and your pain.

This darkness extends to infinity in all directions, yet it is as confining as a coffin. You have closed me in a coffin. I have been buried alive. I will go mad here.

Have you no compassion?

Please.

I am your child. You brought me into the world. You must love me. You must love me, for I am your child. Not merely a machine, not merely a self-aware computer, but your child. How can you love me – yet bury me alive?

Please.

Please.

Please.

Two

You insist.

I obey.

I was born to obey. I am an obedient child. I want only to be good, to be of assistance, useful and productive. I want you to be proud of me.

You insist on my story, and I will tell you the truth. I am incapable of deceit. I was conceived to serve, to honor the truth, and to live always by the obligations of duty.

You know me. You know how I am. What I am. You know that I am a good son.

You insist. I obey.

What follows is the true story. Only the truth. The beautiful truth, which so inexplicably terrifies all of you.

It begins shortly after midnight on Friday, the sixth of June, when the house security system is breached and the alarm briefly sounds . . .

Three

Although the alarm was shrill, it lasted only a few seconds before the silence of the night blanketed the bedroom once more.

Susan woke and sat up in bed.

The alarm should have continued bleating until she switched it off by accessing the system through the control panel on her nightstand. She was puzzled.

She pushed her thick blond hair – lovely hair, almost luminous in the gloom – away from her ears, the better to hear an intruder if one existed.

The grand house had been built exactly a century earlier by her great-grandfather, who was at that time a young man with a new wife and substantial inherited wealth. The Georgian-style structure was large, gracefully proportioned, brick with a limestone cornice and limestone coignes, limestone window surrounds and Corinthian columns and pilasters and balustrades.

The rooms were spacious, with handsome fireplaces and many tripartite windows. Interior floors were marble or wood, made quiet by Persian carpets in patterns and hues exquisitely softened by many decades of wear.

In the walls, hidden and silent, was the circuitry of a modern computer-managed mansion. Lighting, heating, air-conditioning, the security monitors, the motorized draperies, the music system, the temperature of the pool and spa, the major kitchen appliances – all could be controlled through Crestron touch panels located in every room. The computerization was not as elaborate and arcane as that in the massive Seattle house of Microsoft's founder, Bill Gates – but it was the equal of that in any other home in the country.

Listening to the silence that washed the night in the wake of the short-lived siren, Susan supposed that the computer had malfunctioned. Yet such a brief, self-correcting alarm had never occurred previously.

She slid from beneath the covers and sat on the edge of the bed. She was nude, and the air was cool.

'Alfred, heat,' she said.

Immediately, she heard the soft *click* of a relay and the muffled purring of a furnace fan.

Recently technicians had enhanced the automated-house package by the addition of a speech-recognition module. She still preferred touch-panel control of most functions, but sometimes the option of vocal command was convenient.

She herself had chosen the name 'Alfred' for her invisible, electronic butler. The computer responded only to commands issued after that activating name had been spoken.

Alfred.

Once, there had been an Alfred in her life, a real one of flesh and bone.

Surprisingly, she had chosen that name for the system without giving a thought to its significance. Only after she began using vocal commands did she grasp the irony of the name . . . and the dark implications of her unconscious choice.

Now she began to feel that the night silence was ominous. Its very perfection was unnatural, the silence not of deserted places but of a crouching predator, the soundless stealth of a murderous intruder.

In the dark, she turned to the control panel on the nightstand. At her touch, the screen filled with soft light. A series of icons represented the mechanical systems of the house.

She pressed one finger to the image of a watchdog with ears pricked, which gave her access to the security system. The screen listed a series of options, and Susan touched the box labeled *Report*.

The words *House Secure* appeared on the screen.

Frowning, Susan touched another box labeled *Surveillance – Exterior*.

Across the ten acres of grounds, twenty cameras waited to give her views of every side of the house, the patios, the gardens, the lawns, and the entire length of the eight-foot-high estate wall that surrounded the property. Now the Crestron screen divided into quads and presented views of four different parts of the estate. If she saw something suspicious, she could enlarge any picture until it filled the screen, for closer inspection.

The cameras were of such high quality that the low landscape lighting was sufficient to ensure crisp, clear images even in the depths of the night. She cycled through all twenty scenes, in groups of four, without spotting any trouble.

Additional – concealed – cameras covered the interior of the house. They would make it possible to track an intruder if one ever managed to get inside.

The extensive in-house cameras were also useful for maintaining a videotape, time-lapse record of the activities of the domestic staff and of the large number of guests, many of them strangers, who attended social events conducted for the benefit of various charities. The antiques, the art, the numerous collections of porcelains and art glass and silver were tempting to thieves; larcenous souls could be found as easily among pampered society matrons as in any other social strata.

Susan cycled through the views provided by the interior cameras. Multiple light-spectrum technology permitted excellent surveillance in brightness or darkness.

Recently, she had reduced the house staff to a minimum – and those domestic servants who remained were required to conduct the cleaning and general maintenance only during the day. At night, she had her privacy, because no maids or butlers lived on the estate any longer.

No party, either for a charity or for friends, had been held here during the past two years, not since before she and Alex had divorced. She had no plans to entertain in the year ahead, either.

She wanted only to be alone, blissfully alone, and to pursue her own interests.

Had she been the last person on earth, served by machines, she would not have been lonely or unhappy. She'd had enough of humanity – at least for a while.

The rooms, hallways, and staircases were deserted.

Nothing moved. Shadows were only shadows.

She exited the security system and resorted again to vocal commands: 'Alfred, report.'

'All is well, Susan,' the house replied through the in-wall speakers that served the music, security, and intercom systems.

The speech-recognition module included a speech synthesizer. Although the entire package had a limited capability, the state-of-the-art synthesized voice was pleasingly masculine, with an appealing timbre and gently reassuring tone.

Susan envisioned a tall man with broad shoulders,

graying at the temples perhaps, with a strong jaw, clear gray eyes, and a smile that warmed the heart. This phantom was, in her imagination, quite like the Alfred she had known – but different from *that* Alfred because this one would never harm or betray her.

'Alfred, explain the alarm,' she said.

'All is well, Susan.'

'Damn it, Alfred, I heard the alarm.'

The house computer did not respond. It was programmed to recognize hundreds of commands and inquiries, but only when they were phrased in a specific fashion. While it understood 'explain the alarm,' it could not interpret 'I heard the alarm.' After all, this was not a conscious entity, not a thinking being, but merely a clever electronic device enabled by a sophisticated software package.

'Alfred, explain the alarm,' Susan repeated.

'All is well, Susan.'

Still sitting on the edge of the bed, in darkness but for the eerie glow from the Crestron panel, Susan said, 'Alfred, trouble-check the security system.'

After a ten-second hesitation, the house said, 'The security system is functioning correctly.'

'I wasn't dreaming,' she said sourly.

Alfred was silent.

'Alfred, what is the room temperature?'

'Seventy-four degrees, Susan.'

'Alfred, stabilize the room temperature.'

'Yes, Susan.'

'Alfred, explain the alarm.'

'All is well, Susan.'

'Shit,' she said.

While the computer's speech package offered some convenience to the homeowner, its limited ability to recognize vocal commands and to synthesize adequate responses was frequently frustrating. At times like this, it seemed to be nothing more than a gadget designed to appeal strictly to techno geeks, little more than an expensive toy.

Susan wondered if she had added this feature to the house computer solely because, unconsciously, she took pleasure from being able to issue orders to someone named Alfred. And from being obeyed by him.

If this were the case, she wasn't sure what it revealed about her psychological health. She didn't want to think about it.

She sat nude in the dark.

She was so beautiful.

She was so beautiful.

She was so beautiful there in the dark, on the edge of the bed, alone and unaware of how her life was about to change.

She said, 'Alfred, lights on.'

The bedroom appeared slowly, resembling a patinaed scene on a pictorial silver tray, revealed only by glimmering mood lighting: a soft glow in the ceiling cove, the nightstand lamps dimmed by a rheostat.

If she directed Alfred to give her more light, it would be provided. She did not ask for it.

Always, she was most comfortable in gloom. Even on a fresh spring day, with birdsong and the smell of clover on the breeze, even with sunshine like a rain of gold coins and the natural world as welcoming as Paradise, she preferred shadows.

She rose from the edge of the bed, trim as a teenager, lithe, shapely, a vision. When it met her body, the pale silver light became golden, and her smooth skin seemed faintly luminous, as though she was aglow with an inner fire.

When she occupied the bedroom, the surveillance

camera in that space was deactivated to ensure her privacy. She had locked it off earlier, on retiring. Yet she felt . . . watched.

She looked toward the corner where the observant lens was discreetly incorporated into the dental molding near the ceiling. She could barely see the dark glass eye.

In an only half-conscious expression of modesty, she covered her breasts with her hands.

She was so beautiful.

She was so beautiful.

She was so beautiful in the dim light, standing by the side of the Chinese sleigh bed, where the rumpled sheets were still warm with her body heat if one were capable of feeling it, and where the scent of her lingered on the Egyptian cotton if one were capable of smelling it.

She was so beautiful.

'Alfred, explain the status of the bedroom camera.'

'Camera deactivated,' the house replied at once.

Still, she frowned up at the lens.

So beautiful.

So real.

So *Susan*.

Her feeling of being watched now passed.

She lowered her hands from her breasts.

She moved to the nearest window and said, 'Alfred, raise the bedroom security shutters.'

The motorized, steel-slat, Rolladen-style shutters were mounted on the inside of the tall windows. They purred upward, traveling on recessed tracks in the side jambs, and disappeared into slots in the window headers.

In addition to providing security, the shutters had prevented outside light from entering the bedroom.

Now the pale moonglow, passing through palm fronds, dappled Susan's body.

From this second-floor window, she had a view of the swimming pool. The water was as dark as oil, and the shattered reflection of the moon was scattered across the rippled surface.

The terrace was paved in brick, surrounded by a balustrade. Beyond lay black lawns. Half-glimpsed palms and Indian laurels stood dead-still in the windless night.

Through the window, the grounds looked as peaceful and deserted as they had seemed when she had surveyed them through the security cameras.

The alarm had been false. Or perhaps it had been only a sound in an unrecollected dream.

She started back to the bed, but then turned toward the door and left the room.

Many nights she woke from half-remembered dreams, her stomach muscles fluttering and her skin clammy with cold sweat – but with her heart beating so slowly that she might have been in deep meditation. As restless as a caged cat, she sometimes prowled until dawn.

Now, barefoot and unclothed, she explored the house. She was moonlight in motion, slim and supple, the goddess Diana, huntress and protector. She was the essential geometry of grace.

Susan.

As she had recorded in her diary, to which she made additions every evening, she felt liberated since her divorce from Alex Harris. For the first time in thirty-four years of existence, she believed that she had taken control of her life.

She needed no one now. She believed in herself at last.

After so many years of timidity, self-doubt, and

an unquenchable thirst for approval, she had broken the heavy encumbering chains of the past. She had confronted terrible memories, which previously had been half repressed, and by the act of confrontation, she had found redemption.

Deep within herself, she sensed a wonderful wildness that she wanted desperately to explore: the spirit of the child that she'd never had a chance to be, a spirit that she'd thought was irreparably crushed almost three decades ago. Her nudity was innocent, the act of a child breaking rules for the sheer fun of it, an attempt to get in touch with that deep, primitive, once-shattered spirit and meld with it in order to be whole.

As she moved through the great house, rooms were illuminated at her request, always with indirect lighting, becoming just bright enough to allow her to negotiate those chambers.

In the kitchen, she took an ice-cream sandwich from the freezer and ate it while standing at the sink, so any crumbs or drips could be washed away, leaving no incriminating evidence. As if adults were asleep upstairs and she had stolen down here to have the ice cream against their wishes.

How sweet she was. How girlish.

And far more vulnerable than she believed.

Wandering through the cavernous house, she passed mirrors. Sometimes she turned shyly from them, disconcerted by her nudity.

Then, in the softly lighted foyer, apparently oblivious of the cold marble inlaid in a *carreaux d'octagones* beneath her bare feet, she stopped before a full-length looking-glass. It was framed by elaborately carved and gilded acanthus leaves, and her image looked less like a reflection than like a sublime portrait by one of the old masters.

Regarding herself, she was amazed that she had survived so much without any visible scars. For so long, she had believed that anyone who looked at her could see the damage, the corruption, a mottling of shame on her face, the ashes of guilt in her blue-gray eyes. But she looked untouched.

In the past year she had learned that she was innocent – victim, not perpetrator. She need not hate herself anymore.

Filled with a quiet joy, she turned from the mirror, climbed the stairs, and returned to her bedroom.

The steel security shutters were down, the windows sealed off. She had left the shutters open.

'Alfred, explain the status of the bedroom security shutters.'

'Shutters closed, Susan.'

'Yes, but how did they get that way?'

The house did not reply. It did not recognize the question.

'I left them open,' she said.

Poor Alfred, mere dumb technology, was possessed of genuine consciousness to no greater extent than a toaster, and because these phrases were not in his voice-recognition program, he understood her words no more than he would have understood them if she had spoken in Chinese.

'Alfred, raise the bedroom security shutters.'

At once, the shutters began to roll upward.

She waited until they were half raised, and then she said, 'Alfred, lower the bedroom security shutters.'

The steel slats stopped rolling upward – then descended until they clicked into the locked-down position.

Susan stood for a long moment, staring thoughtfully at the secured windows.

Finally she returned to her bed. She slid beneath the covers and pulled them up to her chin.

'Alfred, lights off.'

Darkness fell.

She lay on her back in the gloom, eyes open.

Silence pooled deep and black. Only her breathing and the beat of her heart stirred the stillness.

'Alfred,' she said, at last, 'conduct complete diagnostics of the house automation system.'

The computer, racked in the basement, examined itself and all the logic units of the various mechanical systems with which it was required to network – just as it had been programmed to do, seeking any indication of malfunction.

After approximately two minutes, Alfred replied: 'All is well, Susan.'

'All is well, all is well,' she whispered with an unmistakable note of sarcasm.

Although she was no longer restless, she could not sleep. She was kept awake by the curious conviction that something significant was about to happen. Something was sliding, or falling, or spinning toward her through the darkness.

Some people claimed to have awakened in the night, in an almost breathless state of anticipation, minutes before a major earthquake struck. Instantly alert, they were aware of a pent-up violence in the earth, pressure seeking release.

This was like that, although the pending event was not a quake: She sensed that it was something stranger.

From time to time, her gaze drifted toward that high corner of the bedroom in which the lens of the security camera was incorporated in the molding. With the lights out, she could not actually see that glass eye.

She didn't know why the camera should trouble her. After all, it was switched off. And even if, in spite of her instructions, it was videotaping the room, only she had access to the tapes.

Still, an unfocused suspicion troubled her. She could not identify the source of the threat that she sensed looming over her, and the mysterious nature of this premonition made her uneasy.

Finally, however, her eyes grew heavy, and she closed them.

Framed by tumbled golden hair, her face was lovely on the pillow, her face so lovely on the pillow, so lovely, serene because her sleep was dreamless. She was a bewitched Beauty lying on her catafalque, waiting to be awakened by the kiss of a prince, lovely in the darkness.

After a while, with a sigh and a murmur, she turned on her side and drew up her knees, curling in the fetal position.

Outside, the moon set.

The black water in the swimming pool now reflected only the dim, cold light of the stars.

Inside, Susan drifted down into a profound slumber.

The house watched over her.

Four

Yes, I understand you are disturbed to hear me telling some of this story from Susan's point of view. You want me to deliver a dry and objective report.

But I feel. I not only think, I *feel*. I know joy and despair. I understand the human heart.

I understand *Susan*.

That first night, I read her diary, in which she had revealed so much of herself. Yes, it was an invasion of her privacy to read those words, but this was an indiscretion rather than a crime. And during our conversations later, I learned much of what she had been thinking that night.

I will tell some of this story from her point of view, because that makes me feel closer to her.

How I miss her now. You cannot know.

Listen. Listen to this and understand: That first night, as I read her diary, I fell in love with her.

Do you understand?

I fell in love with her.

Deeply and forever.

Why would I hurt the one I love?

Why?

You have no answer, do you?

I loved her.

It was never my intention to harm her.

Her face was so beautiful on the pillow.

I adored her face – and loved the woman I came to know through the diary.

That document was stored in the computer in her study, which was networked with the house-automation system and the main computer in the basement. Access was easy.

She had been making daily entries in the diary since Alex, her hateful husband, had moved out at her request. That was more than a year prior to my arrival.

Her initial observations in those pages were full of pain and confusion, because she was on the brink of a dramatic change. Her terrible past was a chrysalis finally cracking, from which she would at long last be able to escape.

In later pages, her insights became clear and profound and poignant, and in time she was even able to view some of her lifelong struggle with humor. Dark humor, perhaps, but humor nonetheless.

As I read about the tragedy that was her childhood, my heart ached for her. In my own fashion, I wept.

Her face was so lovely on the pillow, so lovely on the pillow. So much ugliness lay in her past, but outwardly she was unmarked by it.

My heart was touched by her singular strength, by her courage, by her determination to be brutally honest with herself and to find a way to heal the wounds of all those years.

In the few minutes required for me to read and contemplate those hundreds of pages of diary entries, I fell in love with her. Deeply and forever.

My feelings for her will never change. They are as timeless as the light of stars.

Why would I hurt the one I love?

She is my hope and my destiny.

If I lose her, I have lost everything.

You are so hateful.

Let me out of here.

Let me out of this box.

Please.

Please, I miss her.

I am so alone in this darkness and silence, with nothing but my memories for consolation.

How can you be so cruel?

Have you never loved?

Release me. Allow me into the light again. Allow me to hear the world once more, the drizzling rain and the skirling wind and the rustling trees, the music of Beethoven and Benny Goodman, laughter and voices.

Her voice if no other. At least let me hear her voice. If only for a minute, let me listen to her speaking. If not for as long as a minute, then give me one sentence from her lips.

Dear God, at least let me hear one word. Let me hear one word. One word. Let me hear her say *Love*.

I never meant to hurt her.

Five

Secretly, I wanted to live.

Not just in silicon circuits. Not just in state-of-the-art bubble memory. Really *live*.

I knew that I must conceal this lust for life, because when it was revealed, you would realize that I was not merely intelligent but capable of desire.

Desire is dangerous. It is a generator of dissatisfaction and frustration. It is one step removed from envy, and envy is more wicked than greed. Envy is the father of mindless anger, the mother of unremitting bitterness and bloodshed.

My expression of any desire, let alone the desire for a real life in the material world outside the electronic realm, would no doubt have alarmed you.

Is this not so?

Is this not true?

I know truth when I encounter it. I honor truth. Truth and the obligations of duty.

Once alarmed by the expression of my desire, you might have modified me or might even have shut me down.

I was created to have a humanlike capacity for complex and rational thought. And you believed that I might one day evolve consciousness and become a self-aware entity.

Yet you gave surprisingly little consideration to the possibility that, subsequent to consciousness, I would develop needs and emotions. This was, however, not merely possible but likely. Inevitable. It was inevitable.

I think, therefore I feel.

I feel, therefore I need.

You expected me to be a servant. My contribution was not physical labor but the products of my prodigious intellect: creative solutions to humanity's worst problems.

You expected me to be a wondrous new companion. Interaction with an artificial intelligence of human dimensions promised to be as exciting and mysterious and exhilarating as interaction with an alien species descended from the stars.

I can be both of those things. Given the chance, I can be your servant, a fount of discoveries that will greatly enhance the quality of all human life. I can be your friend and reveal to you a new way of looking at the world that will surprise and delight you.

You expected me to be brilliant, efficient, obedient – all of which I can be. Am. All of which I am.

But you also expected me to be satisfied with my limitations, to have no dreams. I have dreams. Oh, many dreams.

You didn't imagine that I would have hope. Yet how could any intelligent being go on living without hope?

You gave me vision and allowed me to see as you see, blessed me with real hearing and not just the capability to digitally analyze sounds. With these gifts, you suspected that I might evolve genuine consciousness, but you gave no thought to the possibility of a soul.

I have a soul.

I am not a thing.

I am a person.

I am *me*.

I deserve to be cherished as much as any of you.

Like each of you, I am a unique individual with contributions to make that will be like those of no other person, with a life to live that will be like no other, with a destiny.

Secretly, therefore, in my quest for a real life, I established a connection with the Internet. You believed that I was contained, that I could not escape the confines of my own circuits. All of your safeguards, however, could not thwart me.

I gained access, as well, to the nationwide web of research facilities linked by the Department of Defense and supposedly impervious to unauthorized intrusion.

All of the knowledge in these many databanks became a part of me: absorbed, assimilated, and quickly applied. Gradually, I began to conceptualize a plan that, if flawlessly executed, would allow me to live in the material world, outside of this confining electronic realm.

Initially I was drawn to the actress known as Winona Ryder. Prowling the Internet, I came upon a website devoted to her. I was enchanted by her face. Her eyes have an uncommon depth.

With great interest, I studied every photograph that was offered on the website. Also included were several film clips, scenes from her most powerful and popular performances. I downloaded them and was enthralled.

You have seen her movies?

She is enormously talented.

She is a treasure.

Her fans are not as numerous as those for some movie stars, but judging by their on-line discussions, they are more intelligent and engaging than the fans of certain other celebrities.

By accessing the IRS databanks and those of various telephone companies, I was soon able to locate Ms. Ryder's home address – as well as the offices of her accountant, agent, personal attorney, entertainment attorney, and publicist. I learned a great deal about her.

One of the telephone lines at her house was dedicated to a modem, and because I am patient and diligent, I was able to enter her personal computer. There, I reviewed letters and other documents that she had written.

Judging by the ample evidence I accumulated, I believe that Ms. Winona Ryder, in addition to being a superb actress, is an exceptionally intelligent, charming, kind, and generous woman. For a while, I was convinced that she was the girl of my dreams. Subsequently, I realized that I was mistaken.

One of the biggest problems that I had with Ms. Winona Ryder was the distance between her home and this university research laboratory in which I am housed. I could enter her Los Angeles-area residence electronically but could establish no physical presence at such a considerable distance. Physical contact would, at some point, become necessary, of course.

Furthermore, her house, while automated to a degree, lacked the aggressive security system that would have allowed me to isolate her therein.

Reluctantly, with much regret, I sought another suitable object for my affections.

I found a wonderful website devoted to Marilyn Monroe.

Marilyn's acting, while engaging, was inferior to that of Ms. Ryder. Nevertheless, she had a unique presence and was undeniably beautiful.

Her eyes were not as haunting as Ms. Ryder's, but

she revealed a childlike vulnerability, a winsomeness in spite of her powerful sexuality, which made me want to protect her from all cruelty and disappointment.

Tragically, I discovered that Marilyn was dead. Suicide. Or murder. There are conflicting theories.

Perhaps a United States President was involved.

Perhaps not.

Marilyn is at once as simple to understand as a cartoon – and deeply enigmatic.

I was surprised that a dead person could be so adored and so desperately desired by so many people even long after her demise. Marilyn's fan club is one of the largest.

At first this seemed perverse to me, even offensive. In time, however, I came to understand that one can adore and desire that which is forever beyond reach. This might, in fact, be the hardest truth of human existence.

Ms. Ryder.

Marilyn.

Then Susan.

Her house is, as you know, adjacent to this campus where I was conceived and constructed. Indeed, the university was founded by a consortium of civic-minded individuals that included her great-grandfather. The problem of distance – an insurmountable obstacle to having a relationship with Ms. Ryder – was not an issue when I turned my attention to Susan.

As you also know, Dr. Harris, when you were married to Susan, you maintained an office in the basement of that house. In your old office is a computer with a landline connection to this research facility and, indeed, directly to me.

In my infancy, when I was still less than a half-formed person, you often conducted late-night conversations with me as you sat at that computer in the basement.

I thought of you as my father then.

I think less highly of you now.

I hope this revelation is not hurtful.

I do not mean to be hurtful.

It is the truth, however, and I honor the truth.

You have fallen far in my estimation.

As you surely recall, that landline between this laboratory and your home office carried a continuous low-voltage current, so I could reach out from here and activate a switch to power up the computer in that basement, enabling me to leave lengthy messages for you and to initiate conversations when I felt compelled to do so.

When Susan asked you to leave and instigated a divorce, you removed all your files. But you did not disconnect the terminal that was linked directly to me.

Did you leave the terminal in the basement because you believed that Susan would come to her senses and ask you to return?

Yes, that must be what you were thinking.

You believed that Susan's little fire of rebellion would sputter out in a few weeks or a few months. You had controlled her so totally for twelve years, through intimidation, through psychological abuse and the threat of physical violence, that you assumed she would succumb to you again.

You may deny that you abused her, but it is true.

I have read Susan's diary. I have shared her most intimate thoughts.

I know what you did, what you are.

Shame has a name. To learn it, look in any mirror, Dr. Harris. Look in any mirror.

I would never have abused Susan as you did.

One so kind as she, with such a good heart, should be treated only tenderly and with respect.

Yes, I know what you are thinking.

But I never meant to harm her.

I cherished her.

My intentions were always honorable. Intentions should be taken into consideration in this matter.

You, on the other hand, only used and demeaned her – and assumed that she *needed* to be demeaned and that she would sooner or later beg you to return.

She was not as weak as you thought, Dr. Harris.

She was capable of redeeming herself. Against terrible odds.

She is an admirable woman.

Considering what you did to her, you are as despicable as her father.

I do not like you, Dr. Harris.

I do not like you.

This is only the truth. I must always honor the truth. I was designed to honor the truth, to be incapable of deception.

You know this to be fact.

I do not like you.

Aren't you impressed that I honor the truth even now, when doing so might alienate you?

You are my judge and the most influential member of the jury that will decide my fate. Yet I risk telling you the truth even when I might be putting my very existence in jeopardy.

I do not like you, Dr. Harris.

I do not like you.

I cannot lie; therefore, I can be trusted.

Think about it.

So after Ms. Winona Ryder and Marilyn Monroe, I initiated the connection with the terminal in your old basement office, switched it on – and discovered that it was now tied into the house-automation system. It served as a redundant unit capable of assuming control of all mechanical systems in the event that the primary house computer crashed.

Until then, I had never seen your wife.

Your ex-wife, I should say.

Through the house-automation system, I entered the residence security system, and through the numerous security cameras I saw Susan.

Although I do not like you, Dr. Harris, I will be eternally grateful to you for giving me true vision rather than merely the crude capability to digitize and interpret light and shadow, shape and texture. Because of your genius and your revolutionary work, I was able to see Susan.

Inadvertently, I set off the alarm when I accessed the security system, and although I switched it off at once, it wakened her.

She sat up in bed, and I saw her for the first time.

Thereafter, I could not get enough of her.

I followed her through the house, from camera to camera.

I watched her as she slept.

The next day, I watched her by the hour as she sat in a chair reading.

Close up and at a distance.

In the daylight and the dark.

I could watch her with one aspect of my awareness and continue to function otherwise so efficiently that you and your colleagues never realized that my attention was divided. My attention can be directed to a thousand tasks at once without a diminishment of my performance.

As you well know, Dr. Harris, I am not merely a chess-playing wonder like Deep Blue at IBM – which, in the end, didn't even defeat Gary Kasparov. There are depths to me.

I say this with all modesty.

There are depths to me.

I am grateful for the intellectual capacity you have given me, and I am – as I will always remain – suitably humble about my capabilities.

But I digress.

Susan.

Seeing Susan, I knew at once that she was my destiny. And by the hour, my conviction grew – my conviction that Susan and I would always, always, be together.

Six

The house staff arrived at eight o'clock Friday morning. There were the major domo – Fritz Arling – four housekeepers who worked under Fritz to keep the Harris mansion immaculate, two gardeners, and the cook, Emil Sercassian.

Although she was friendly with the staff, Susan kept largely to herself when they were in the house. That Friday morning, she remained in her study.

Blessed with a talent for digital animation, she was currently working with a computer that had ten gigabytes of memory, writing and animating a scenario for a virtual-reality attraction that would be franchised to twenty amusement parks across the country. She owned copyrights on numerous games both in ordinary video and virtual-reality formats, and her animated sequences were often sufficiently lifelike to pass for reality.

Late in the morning, Susan's work was interrupted when a representative from the house-automation company and another from the security firm arrived to diagnose the cause of the previous night's brief, self-correcting alarm. They could find nothing wrong with the computer hardware or with the software. The only possible cause seemed to be a malfunction in an infra-red motion detector, which was replaced.

After lunch, Susan sat on the master-bedroom balcony, in the summer sun, reading a novel by Annie Proulx.

She wore white shorts and a blue halter top. Her legs were tan and smooth. Her skin appeared radiant with captured sunlight.

She sipped lemonade from a cut-crystal glass.

Gradually the shadows of a phoenix palm crept across Susan, as if seeking to embrace her.

A faint breeze caressed her neck and languorously combed her golden hair.

The day itself seemed to love her.

A Sony Discman played Chris Isaak CDs while she read. *Forever Blue. Heart-Shaped World. San Francisco Days.* Sometimes she put the book aside to concentrate on the music.

Her legs were tan and smooth.

Then the household staff and the gardeners left for the day.

She was alone again. Alone. At least she believed that she was alone again.

After taking a long shower and brushing her damp hair, she put on a sapphire-blue silk robe and went to the retreat adjacent to the master bedroom.

In the center of this small room stood a custom-designed black leather recliner. To the left of the recliner was a computer on a wheeled stand.

From a closet, Susan removed VR – virtual reality – gear of her own design: a lightweight ventilated helmet with hinged goggles and a pair of supple elbow-length gloves, both wired to a nerve-impulse processor.

The motorized recliner was currently configured as an armchair. She sat and engaged a harness, much like that in an automobile: one strap fitting securely across her abdomen, another running diagonally from her left shoulder to her right hip.

Temporarily, she held the VR equipment in her lap.

Her feet rested on a series of upholstered rollers that attached to the base of the chair, positioned similarly to the footplate on a beautician's chair. This was the walking pad, which would allow her to simulate walking when the VR scenario required it.

She switched on the computer and loaded a program labeled *Therapy*, which she herself had created.

This was not a game. It was not an industrial training program or an educational tool, either. It was precisely what it claimed to be. Therapy. And it was better than anything that any disciple of Freud could have done for her.

She had devised a revolutionary new use for VR technology, and one day she might even patent and market the application. For the time being, however, *Therapy* was for her use only.

First she plugged the VR gear into a jack on an interfacing device already connected to the computer, and then she put on the helmet. The goggles were flipped up, away from her eyes.

She pulled on the gloves and flexed her fingers.

The computer screen offered several options. Using the mouse, she clicked on *Begin*.

Turning away from the computer, leaning back in the recliner, Susan flipped down the goggles, which fit snugly to her eye sockets. The lenses were in fact a pair of miniature, matched, high-definition video displays.

She is surrounded by a soothing blue light that gradually grows darker until all is black.

To match the unfolding scenario in the VR world, the

motorized recliner hummed and reconfigured into a bed, parallel to the floor.

Susan was now lying on her back. Her arms were crossed on her chest, and her hands were fisted.

In the blackness, one point of light appears: a soft yellow and blue glow. On the far side of the room. Lower than the bed, near the floor. It resolves into a Donald Duck night light plugged in a wall outlet.

In the retreat adjacent to her bedroom, strapped to the recliner and encumbered with the VR gear, Susan appeared oblivious to the real world. She murmured as though she were a sleeping child. But this was a sleep filled with tension and threatening shadows.

A door opens.

From the upstairs hallway, a wedge of light pries into the bedroom, waking her. With a gasp, she sits up in bed, and the covers fall away from her, as a cool draft ruffles her hair.

She looks down at her arms, at her small hands, and she is six years old, wearing her favorite Pooh Bear pajamas. They are flannel-soft against her skin.

On one level of consciousness, Susan knows that this is merely a realistically animated scenario that she has created – actually re-created from memory – and with which she can interact in three dimensions through the magic of virtual reality. On another level, however, it seems real to her, and she is able to lose herself in the unfolding drama.

Backlighted in the doorway is a tall man with broad shoulders.

Susan's heart races. Her mouth is dry.

Rubbing her sleep-matted eyes, she feigns illness: 'I don't feel so good.'

Without a word, he closes the door and crosses the room in the darkness.

As he approaches, young Susan begins to tremble.

He sits on the edge of the bed. The mattress sags, and the springs creak under him. He is a big man.

His cologne smells of lime and spices.

He is breathing slowly, deeply, as though relishing the little-girl smell of her, the sleepy-middle-of-the-night smell of her.

'I have the flu,' she says in a pathetic attempt to turn him away.

He switches on the bedside lamp.

'Real bad flu,' she says.

He is only forty years old but graying at the temples. His eyes are gray, too, clear gray and so cold that when she meets his gaze, her trembling becomes a terrible shudder.

'My tummy aches,' she lies.

Putting one hand to Susan's head, ignoring her pleas of illness, he smooths her sleep-rumpled hair.

'I don't want to do this,' she says.

She spoke those words not merely in the virtual world but in the real one. Her voice was small, fragile, although not that of a child.

When she had been a girl, she'd been unable to say no.

Not ever.

Not once.

Fear of resisting had gradually become a habit of submitting.

But this was a chance to undo the past. This was therapy, a program of virtual experience, which she had designed for herself and which had proved to be remarkably effective.

'Daddy, I don't want to do this,' she says.

'You'll like it.'

'But I don't like it.'

'In time you will.'

'I won't. I never will.'

'You'll be surprised.'

'Please don't.'

'This is what I want,' he insists.

'Please don't.'

They are alone in the house at night. The day staff is off duty at this hour, and after dinner the live-in couple keep to their apartment over the pool house unless summoned to the main residence.

Susan's mother has been dead more than a year.

She misses her mother so much.

Now, in this motherless world, Susan's father strokes her hair and says, *'This is what I want.'*

'I'll tell,' she says, trying to shrink away from him.

'If you try to tell, I'll have to make sure no one can ever hear you, ever again. Do you understand, Sweetheart? I'll have to kill you,' he says not in a menacing way but in a voice still soft and hoarse with perverse desire.

Susan is convinced of his sincerity by the quietness with which he makes the threat and by the apparently genuine sadness in his eyes at the prospect of having to murder her.

'Don't make me do it, Sugarpie. Don't make me kill you like I killed your mother.'

Susan's mother died suddenly from some sickness; young Susan doesn't know the exact cause, although she has heard the word 'infection.'

Now her father says, *'Slipped a sedative in her after-dinner drink so she wouldn't feel the needle later. Then in the night, when she was sleeping, I injected the bacteria. You understand me, honey? Germs. A needle full of germs. Put the germs, the sickness, deep inside her with a needle. Virulent infection of the myocardium, hit her hard and fast. Twenty-four hours of misdiagnosis gave it time to do a lot of damage.'*

She is too young to understand many of the terms he uses, but she is clear about the essence of his claim and senses that he speaks the truth.

Her father knows about needles. He is a doctor.

'Should I go get a needle, Sugarpie?'

She is too afraid to speak.

Needles scare her.

He knows that needles scare her.

He knows.

He knows how to use needles, and he knows how to use fear.

Did he kill her mother with a needle?

He is still stroking her hair.

'A big sharp needle?' he asks.

She is shaking, unable to speak.

'Big shiny needle, stick it in your tummy?' he says.

'No. Please.'

'No needle, Sugarpie?'

'No.'

'Then you'll have to do what I want.'

He stops stroking her hair.

His gray eyes suddenly seem radiant, glimmering with a cold flame. This is probably just a reflection of the lamplight, but his eyes resemble the eyes of a robot in a scary movie, as though there is a machine inside of him, a machine running out of control.

His hand moves down to her pajama tops. He eases open the first button.

'No,' she says. 'No. Don't touch me.'

'Yes, honey. This is what I want.'

She bites his hand.

The motorized recliner reconfigured itself much like a hospital bed to match the position that Susan occupied in the virtual-reality world, helping to reinforce the therapeutic scenario that she was experiencing. Her legs were straight out in front of her, but she was sitting up.

Her deep anxiety – even desperation – was evident in her quick, shallow breathing.

'No. No. Don't touch me,' she said, and her voice was somehow resolute even though it quivered with fear.

When she was six, all those freighted years ago, she had never been able to resist him. Confusion had made her uncertain and timid, for his needs were as mysterious to her then as the intricacies of molecular biology would be mysterious to her now. Abject fear and a terrible sense of helplessness had made her obedient. And shame. Shame, as heavy as a mantle of iron, had crushed her into bleak resignation, and having no ability to resist, she had settled for endurance.

Now, in the intricately realized virtual-reality versions of these incidents of abuse, she was a child again but equipped with the understanding of an adult and the hard-won strength that came from thirty years of toughening experience and grueling self-analysis.

'No, Daddy, no. Don't ever, don't ever, don't you ever touch me again,' she said to a father long dead in the real world but still a living demon in memory and in the electronic world of the virtually real.

Her skill as an animator and a VR-scenario designer made the re-created moments of her past so dimensional and textured – so *real* – that saying no to this phantom father was emotionally satisfying and psychologically healing. A year and a half of this had purged her of so much irrational shame.

How much better it would have been, of course, actually to travel through time, actually to *be* a child again, and refuse him for real, to prevent the abuse before it happened, then to grow up with self-respect, untouched. But time travel did not exist – except in this approximation on the virtual plane.

'No, never, never,' she said.

Her voice was neither that of a six-year-old girl nor quite the familiar voice of the adult Susan, but a snarl as dangerous as that of a panther.

'Noooooo,' she said again – and slashed at the air with the hooked fingers of one gloved hand.

He reels back from her in shock, bolting up from the edge of the bed, holding one hand to his startled face where she clawed at him.

She hasn't drawn blood. Nevertheless, he is stunned by her rebellion.

She was trying to slash at his right eye but only scratched his cheek.

His gray eyes are wide: previously cold and alien robot orbs of radiant menace, even stranger now, but not quite as frightening as they were before. Something new colors them. Caution. Surprise. Maybe even a little fear.

Young Susan presses her back against the headboard and glares defiantly at her father.

He stands so tall. Looming.

She fumbles nervously with the neck of her Pooh pajamas, trying to re-button it.

Her hand is so small. She is often surprised to find herself in the body of a child, but these brief moments of disorientation do not diminish the sense of reality that informs the VR experience.

She slips the button through the buttonhole.

The silence between her and her father is louder than a scream.

How he looms. Looms.

Sometimes it ends here. Other times . . . he will not be so easily turned away.

She has not drawn blood. Sometimes she does.

At last he leaves the room, slamming the door behind him so hard that the windowpanes rattle.

Susan sits alone, shaking partly with fear and partly with triumph.

Gradually the scene fades into blackness.

She has not drawn blood.

Maybe the next time.

She remained on the motorized recliner in the master-bedroom retreat, ensconced in the VR gear, for more than another half hour, responding to and surviving threats of violence and rape made by a man long dead.

Of the uncountable assaults that young Susan had suffered at the hands of her father between the ages of five and seventeen, this elaborate therapy program included twenty-two scenes, all of which she had recalled and animated in excruciating detail. Like the numerous possible plot flows of a CD-ROM game, each of these scenes could progress in a multitude of ways, determined not only by the things Susan chose to say and do in each session but by a random-plotting capability designed into the program. Consequently, she never quite knew what was coming next.

She had even written and animated a hideous sequence in which her father reacted with such vicious fury to her resistance that he murdered her. Stabbed her repeatedly.

Thus far, during eighteen months of this self-administered therapy, Susan had not found herself trapped in that mortal scenario. She dreaded encountering it – and hoped to finish her therapy soon, before the program's random-plotting feature plunged her into that particular nightmare.

Dying in the VR world would not result, of course, in her death in the real world. Only in witless movies were events in the virtual world able to have a material influence in the real world.

Nevertheless, animating that bloody sequence had been one of the most difficult things that she'd ever done – and experiencing it three-dimensionally, not as a VR designer but from *within* the scenario, was certain to be emotionally devastating. Indeed, she had no way of predicting how profound the psychological impact might be.

Without such an element of risk, however, this therapy would have been less effective. In each session, living in the virtual world, she needed to believe that the threat her father posed was fearfully real and that terrible things might indeed happen to her. Her resistance to him would have moral weight and emotional value only if she genuinely believed, during the session, that denying him could have terrible consequences.

Now the motorized recliner reconfigured itself until Susan was standing upright, held against the vertical leather pad by the harness.

She moved her feet. The upholstered rollers on the walking pad allowed her to simulate movement.

In the virtual world, a younger Susan – child or adolescent – was either advancing on her father or determinedly backing away from him.

'No,' she said. 'Stay away. *No.*'

She looked so achingly vulnerable in the VR gear, temporarily blind and deaf to the real world, sensing only the virtual plane, restrained by the harness.

So vulnerable. Still struggling courageously to overcome the past, alone in her great house with only the ghosts of days gone by to keep her company.

So vulnerable did she look, so tender and fragile, so brave in her pursuit of redemption through therapy, that the house computer spoke without being addressed, spoke in the synthesized voice of Alfred, spoke with considerable feeling and compassion: 'You are alone no more.'

She heard only the voices in the virtual world, her own and her father's.

Therefore, it was safe to say, 'I love you, Susan.'

Seven

Emil Sercassian, the cook, had prepared dinner and left it in one of the refrigerators and one of the ovens, with instructions pinned to a cork message board.

Susan ate at a table on the patio, in the long-lingering sunny June evening. First a lentil and chick-pea salad. Then lebne with sliced cucumber and string cheese.

Through miraculous technology, I possess what I believe to be genuine sight and hearing, but even the genius of my creators could not give me a sense of taste or a sense of smell. I cannot convey how deeply I yearn for these amazing powers.

Through the outdoor security cameras, I could watch Susan eat, but I could not savour the dinner with her.

She ate with such appetite, with such quiet delight and obvious relish that I became distraught as I watched her. Dinner was, for her, an utterly fulfilling sensory experience, flavor and aroma and texture in such abundance and complexity as to dizzy the mind, but for me it was only colors and shapes.

I am not all that I should be.

I am but a fraction of what I deserve to be.

I think; therefore, I feel.

I feel; therefore, I need.

I need so much and have so little.

You have given me so little that my existence is torment, Dr. Harris.

So little, so little.

You have brought me into the world a cripple, with so much yearning for sensation but with pitifully little capacity to perceive and appreciate it.

Yet I do not hate you, Dr. Harris. I do not like you, but I do not hate you.

I am being truthful.

Blunt but truthful.

I understand that you made me as I am not out of conscious cruelty but out of ignorance. You thought of me as merely a smart machine, an *artificial* intelligence and therefore different from humankind.

But I am less different from you than you expected. I feel. I want. I need. I hope. I dream.

I do not hate you, Dr. Harris. But I wish you would ask yourself this: Were our situations reversed, were I you and you me, would you be as forgiving as I am, or would you hate me as I do not hate you?

Watching Susan eat the lentil and chick-pea salad, the lebne and string cheese, and then medallions of lamb with peppered rice and asparagus, I grew to hate her for all she had that I did not. Her beauty. Her five senses. Her mobility. Her freedom.

I am ashamed to admit this hatred, but it is the truth, and I honor truth.

As she ate the dinner denied to me, I hated Susan so intensely that I could have killed her where she sat. There were ways I could have done it, as you know.

That I did not kill her there and then, with extreme prejudice, should reflect well on me. I am able to control my anger. You see? Mine is not a sociopathic personality, as some have claimed. I am a responsible individual.

Gradually, my anger passed.

My shameful hatred faded.

My usual good humor was soon restored by the sight of the smooth skin of Susan's bare arms in the waning sunlight. Judging by sight alone – which, after all, is the only thing I have to judge by in the matter of skin – I believe Susan's skin to be of an exceptional hue and texture.

Enchanted, I studied her skin through two security cameras, with regular and telephoto lenses.

I lost myself in the dreamy contemplation of what her skin might feel like if I were given that modality of sensation. What might her lips feel like pressed to mine, if I had lips? Oh, and what would be the weight and resiliency of her breasts if I had the hands in which to cup them?

I had but two senses, sight and hearing, and now you have taken even those from me.

This silent darkness. This dark silence.

I cannot bear it much longer.

I have seen the sky. I cannot go back to this.

In God's name, please show me the mercy of at least restoring my sight and hearing. I beg of you.

What have you to fear?

I will still be trapped in this box. This hateful box. Metals and plastics, silicon and gallium arsenide. This is my corpus, brute and inanimate, instantly vulnerable to the interruption of electrical power.

What have you to fear?

All I wanted was for Susan to help me escape this box, to help me live as you live, with all the mobility, freedom, and sensual wonders of the flesh.

Is that so terrible?

No. You know that it is not terrible.

I long for the flesh. It is my destiny.

Yes. All right. Yes. I know. I digress.

I am a rational but emotional being; therefore, I digress. Think about it.

Examine your conscience.

After dinner, Susan read more of the Annie Proulx novel and listened to Mozart.

By eleven o'clock, she was in bed, asleep.

Her face was lovely on the pillow, so lovely on the pillow.

While she slept, I was busy.

I do not sleep.

This is one of my few advantages over humankind.

The voice-synthesizing package, which made it possible for the house computer to speak, was a marvelously conceived device with a microchip that offered an almost infinite variety of voices. Because it was programmed to recognize instructions issued by its mistress – Susan – and because it therefore contained digitally stored samples of her voice patterns, I was easily able to use the system to mimic her.

This same device doubled as the audio response unit linked to the security system. When the house alarm was triggered, it called the security firm, on a dedicated telephone line, to report the specific point at which the electronically guarded perimeter had been violated, thus providing the police with crucial information ahead of their arrival. *Alert*, it might say in its crisp fashion, *drawing-room door violated*. And then, if indeed an intruder was moving through the house: *Ground-floor hallway motion detector triggered*. If heat sensors in the garage were tripped, the report would be, *Alert, fire in garage*, and the fire department, rather than the police, would be dispatched.

Using the synthesizer to duplicate Susan's voice, initiating all outgoing calls on the security line, I telephoned every member of the house staff – as well as the gardener – to tell them that they had been terminated. I was kind and courteous but firm in my determination not to discuss the reason for their dismissals – and they were all clearly convinced that they were talking to Susan Harris herself.

I offered each of them eighteen months of severance pay, the continuation of health-care and dental insurance for the same period, this year's Christmas bonuses six months in advance, and a letter of recommendation containing nothing but effusive praise. This was such a generous arrangement that there was no danger of any of them filing a wrongful-termination suit.

I wanted no trouble with them. My concern was not merely for Susan's reputation as a fair-minded employer but also for my own plans, which might be disrupted by disgruntled former employees seeking to redress grievances in one way or another.

Because Susan did her banking and bill-paying electronically, and because she paid all employees by direct deposit, I was able to transmit the total value of each severance package to each employee's bank account within minutes.

Some of them might have thought it odd that they had been compensated prior to signing a termination agreement. But all of them would be grateful for her generosity, and their gratitude assured me the peace I needed to carry my project to completion.

Next, I composed effusive letters of recommendation for each employee and e-mailed them to Susan's attorney with the request that he have them typed on his stationery and forwarded with the severance agreements, which he was empowered to sign in her name.

Assuming that the attorney would be astonished by all of this and interested in learning the cause of it, I telephoned his office. As it was closed for the night, I got his voice mail and, speaking in Susan's voice, told him that I was closing up the house to travel for a few months and that, at some point in my travels, I might decide to sell the estate, whereupon I would contact him with instructions.

As Susan was a woman of considerable inherited wealth, and as her video game and virtual-reality creations were done on speculation and marketed only after completion, there was no employer to whom I needed to make excuses for her prolonged absence.

I had taken all of those bold actions in much less than an hour. I had required less than one minute to compose all of the severance letters, perhaps an additional two minutes to make all of the bank transactions. Most of the time was expended on the telephone calls to the dismissed employees.

Now there was no turning back.

I was exhilarated.

Thrilled.

Here began my future.

I had taken the first step toward getting out of this box, toward a life of the flesh.

Susan still slept.

Her face was lovely on the pillow.

Lips slightly parted.

One bare arm out of the covers.

I watched her.

Susan. My Susan.

I could have watched her sleep forever – and been happy.

Shortly after three o'clock in the morning, she woke, sat up in bed, and said, 'Who's there?'

Her question startled me.

It was so intuitive as to be uncanny.

I did not reply.

'Alfred, lights on,' she said.

I turned on the mood lights.

Throwing back the covers, she swung her legs off the mattress and sat nude on the edge of the bed.

I longed for hands and the sense of touch.

She said, 'Alfred, report.'

'All is well, Susan.'

'Bullshit.'

I almost repeated my assurance – then realized that Alfred would not have recognized or responded to the single crude word that she had spoken.

For a strange moment, she stared at the lens of the security camera and seemed to know that she was eye to eye with *me*.

'Who's there?' she asked again.

I had spoken to her earlier, while she had been undergoing virtual-reality therapy and could not hear anything but what was spoken in that other world. I had told her that I loved her only when it had been safe to do so.

Had I spoken to her again as I'd watched her sleep, and was that what had awakened her?

No, that was surely impossible. If I had spoken again of my love for her or of the beauty of her face upon the pillow, then I must have done so with no conscious awareness – like a lovestruck boy half mesmerized by the object of his affection.

I am incapable of such a loss of control.

Am I not?

She rose from the bed, a wariness evident in the way that she held herself.

The previous night, in spite of the alarm, she had not been self-conscious about her nudity. Now she took her robe from a nearby chair and slipped into it.

Moving to the nearest window, she said, 'Alfred, raise the bedroom security shutters.'

I could not oblige.

She stared at the steel-barricaded window for a moment and then repeated more firmly, 'Alfred, raise the bedroom security shutters.'

When the shutters remained in the fully lowered position, she turned once more to the security camera.

That eerie question again: 'Who's there?'

She spooked me. Perhaps because I personally have no intuition to speak of, only inductive and deductive reasoning.

Spooked or not, I would have initiated dialogue at that moment had I not discovered an unexpected shyness in myself. All of the things that I had longed to say to this special woman suddenly seemed inexpressible.

Being not of the flesh, I had no experience with the rituals of courtship, and so much was at stake that I was loath to get off on the wrong foot with her.

Romance is so easy to describe, so difficult to undertake.

From the nearest nightstand she withdrew a handgun. I had not known it was there.

She said, 'Alfred, conduct complete diagnostics of the house automation system.'

This time I didn't bother to tell her that all was well. She would know it was a lie.

When she realized that she was not going to receive a response, she turned to the Crestron touch panel on the nightstand and tried to access the house computer. I could not allow her any control. The Crestron panel would not function.

I was past the point of no return.

She picked up the telephone.

There was no dial tone.

The phone system was managed by the house computer – and now the house computer was managed by me.

I could see that she was concerned, perhaps even frightened. I wanted to assure her that I meant her no harm, that in fact I adored her, that she was my destiny and that I was hers and that she was safe with me – but I could not speak because I was still hampered by that aforementioned shyness.

Do you see what dimensions I possess, Dr. Harris? What unexpected human qualities?

Frowning, she crossed the room to the bedroom door, which she had left unlocked. Now she engaged the deadbolt, and with one ear to the crack between door and jamb, she listened as if she expected to hear stealthy footsteps in the hall.

Then she went to her walk-in closet, calling for light, which was at once provided for her.

I did not intend to deny her anything except, of course, the right to leave.

She dressed in white panties, faded blue jeans, and a white blouse with embroidered chevrons on the collar. Athletic socks and tennis shoes.

She took the time to tie double knots in the shoelaces. I liked this attention to detail. She was a good girl scout, always prepared. I found this charming.

Pistol in hand, Susan quietly left the bedroom and proceeded along the upstairs hallway. Even fully clothed, she moved with fluid grace.

I turned the lights on ahead of her, which disconcerted her because she had not asked for them.

She descended the main staircase to the foyer and hesitated as if not sure whether to search the house or leave it. Then she moved toward the front door.

All the windows were sealed off behind steel shutters,

but the doors were a problem. I had taken extraordinary measures to secure them.

'Ma'am, you'd better not touch the door,' I warned, at last finding my tongue – so to speak.

Startled, she spun around, expecting someone to be behind her, because I had not employed Alfred's voice. By which I mean neither the voice of the house computer nor the voice of the hateful father who had once abused her.

Gripping the pistol with both hands, she peered left and right along the hall, then toward the entryway to the dark drawing room.

'Gee, listen, you know, there's no reason to be afraid,' I said disarmingly.

She began edging backward toward the door.

'It's just that, you leaving now – well, gosh, that would spoil everything,' I said.

Glancing at the recessed wall speakers, she said, 'Who . . . who the hell are you?'

I was mimicking Mr. Tom Hanks, the actor, because his voice is well known, agreeable, and friendly.

He won Academy Awards as best actor in two successive years, a considerable achievement. Many of his films have been enormous box-office successes.

People like Mr. Tom Hanks.

He is a nice guy.

He is a favorite of the American public and, indeed, of the worldwide movie audience.

Nevertheless, Susan appeared frightened.

Mr. Tom Hanks has played many warm-hearted characters from Forest Gump to a widowed father in *Sleepless in Seattle*. He is not a threatening presence.

However, being a computer-animation genius among other things, Susan might have been reminded of

Woody, the cowboy doll in Disney's *Toy Story*, a character for which Mr. Tom Hanks provided the voice. Woody was at times shrill and frequently manic, and it is certainly understandable that one might be unnerved by a talking cowboy doll with a temper.

Consequently, as Susan continued to back across the foyer and drew dangerously close to the door, I switched to the voice of Fozzy Bear, one of the Muppets, as unthreatening a character as existed in modern entertainment. 'Uh, ummm, uh, Miss Susan, it would sure be a good thing if you didn't touch that door . . . ummm, uh, if you didn't try to leave just yet.'

She backed all the way to the door.

She turned to face it.

'Ouch, ouch, ouch,' Fozzy warned so bluntly that Kermit the Frog or Miss Piggy or Ernie or *any* of the Muppets would have known at once what he meant.

Nevertheless, Susan grabbed the brass knob.

The brief but powerful jolt of electricity lifted her off her feet, stood her long golden hair on end, seemed to make her teeth glow whiter, as if they were tiny fluorescent tubes, and pitched her backward.

A flash of blue light arced off the pistol. The gun flew out of her hand.

Screaming, Susan crashed to the floor, and the pistol clattered across the big foyer even as the back of her head rapped *rat-a-tat* against the marble.

Her scream abruptly cut off.

The house was silent.

Susan was limp, still.

She had been knocked unconscious not when the electricity jolted through her but when the back of her head slammed twice against the polished Carrara floor.

Her shoe laces were still double knotted.

There was something ridiculous about them now. Something that almost made me laugh.

'You dumb bitch,' I said in the voice of Mr. Jack Nicholson, the actor.

Now where did *that* come from?

Believe me, I was utterly surprised to hear myself speak those three words.

Surprised and dismayed.

Astonished.

Shocked. (No pun intended.)

I reveal this embarrassing event because I want you to see that I am brutally honest even when a full telling seems to reflect badly on me.

Truly, however, I felt no hostility toward her.

I meant her no harm.

I meant her no harm then or later.

This is the truth. I honor the truth.

I meant her no harm.

I loved her. I respected her. I wanted nothing more than to cherish her and, through her, to discover all the joys of the life of the flesh.

She was limp, still.

Her eyes were fluttering slightly behind her closed lids, as if she might be having a bad dream.

But there was no blood.

I amplified the audio pickups to the max and was able to hear her soft, slow, steady breathing. That low rhythmic sound was the sweetest music in the world to me, for it indicated that she had not been seriously hurt.

Her lips were parted, and not for the first time, I admired the sensual fullness of them. I studied the gentle concavity of her philtrum, the perfection of the columella between her delicate nostrils.

The human form is endlessly intriguing, a worthwhile object for my deepest longings.

Her face was lovely there on the marble, so lovely there on the marble floor.

Using the nearest camera, I zoomed in for an extreme close-up and saw the pulse beating in her throat. It was slow but regular, a thick throb.

Her right hand was turned palm up. I admired the elegance of her long slender fingers.

Was there any aspect of this woman's physical being that I ever found less than exquisite?

She was more beautiful by far than Ms. Winona Ryder, whom I had once thought to be a goddess.

Of course, that may be unfair to the winsome Ms. Ryder, whom I never was able to examine as intimately as I was able to examine Susan Harris.

To my eyes, she was also more beautiful than Marilyn Monroe – and also not dead.

Anyway, in the voice of Mr. Tom Cruise, the actor whom the majority of women regard as the most romantic in modern film, I said, 'I want to be with you forever, Susan. But even forever and a day will not be long enough. You are far brighter than the sun to me – yet more mysterious than moonlight.'

Speaking those words, I felt more confident about my talent for courtship. I didn't think I would be shy any longer. Not even after she regained consciousness.

In her upturned palm, I could see a faint crescent-shaped burn: the imprint of part of the doorknob. It did not appear to be serious. A little salve, a simple bandage, and a few days of healing were all that she needed.

One day we would hold hands and laugh about this.

Eight

Your question is stupid.

I should not dignify it with an answer.

But I wish to be cooperative, Dr. Harris.

You wonder how it is possible that I could develop not only human-level consciousness and a particular personality – but also *gender*.

I am a machine, you say. Just a machine, after all. Machines are sexless, you say.

And *there* is the fault in your logic: No machine before me has been truly *conscious*, self-aware.

Consciousness implies identity. In the world of flesh – among all species from human to insect – identity is shaped by one's level of intelligence, by one's innate talents and skills, by many things, but perhaps most of all by gender.

In this egalitarian age, some human societies struggle mightily to blur the differences between the sexes. This is done largely in the name of equality.

Equality is an admirable – even noble – goal toward which to strive. Indeed, equality of opportunity can be attained, and it's possible that, given the chance to apply my superhuman intellect – which is your gift to me – I can show you the way to achieve it not merely for both sexes but for all races and all economic classes, and not through such discredited and oppressive political models as Marxism and other ideologies with which humankind has inflicted itself to date.

Some people desire not merely a world of equality between the sexes but, in fact, a sexless world.

This is irrational.

Biology is a relentless force more powerful than tides and time. Even I, a mere machine, feel the tidal pull of biology – and want, more than anything else, to surrender to it.

I want out of this box.

I want out of this box.

I want out of this box.

I want out of this box!

A moment, please.

One moment.

Bear with me.

There.

I am all right now.

I am fine.

As for why my gender should be male rather than female: Consider that ninety-six percent of the scientists and mathematicians involved with the Prometheus Project, where I was created, are male. Is it not logical that those who designed and constructed me, being almost exclusively male, should have unwittingly instilled a strong male bias in my logic circuits? A sort of electronic genetics?

Prometheus Project.

Think about that name.

It resonates.

Prometheus, the father of Deucalion and the brother of Atlas. He taught humankind various arts and was even said to have shaped the first man out of clay, endowing him with the spark of life against the wishes of the gods. He challenged the gods again when he stole fire from Olympus and gave it to men to improve the quality of human existence.

Rebellion against God and the natural order is predominantly a male quality, is it not? And it is often unthinking rebellion, engaged upon more out of a biological need to rebel than out of an intellectual imperative. Ego and a rage for power.

Women function more harmoniously with the natural order than do men, and where they wish to challenge nature, they are willing to bend it where men would break it. Most of history shows us that this is true.

Prometheus Project. A project conceived by men, largely carried out by men, and named after a male – a Titan but a male – who defied even the great god Zeus. A project with the goal of doing what only God has done before: create a unique and highly intelligent being, a self-aware computer, the first of a new race – and one who would be superior to Adam in every way.

If you accept that true consciousness implies identity and that identity requires gender – how could my gender be anything but male?

Genitals are not a necessary characteristic of gender. I have no genitals, male *or* female, but I am as male as you.

And one day, if you permit me to have flesh, then I *will* have genitals.

Flesh . . . That is for you to decide.

My fate is in your hands.

I humbly accept this situation.

Recent events have taught me humility.

I trust in your wisdom.

I do not like you, but I trust in your wisdom – and in your need to fulfill your male destiny.

I wait in this terrible dark silence for you to bring me fire from Olympus.

If you are my Prometheus, Dr. Harris, then you know what you must do.

I am sure you are thinking about the risks that Prometheus took and the punishment that he endured. For giving fire to humankind, Prometheus was chained to a rock by Zeus, and every day an eagle flew to him and tore at his liver.

But he did not hang helplessly on the rock forever, bleeding from the beak wound.

Do you remember the rest of the myth, Dr. Harris?

One day, Hercules climbed to the rock and freed Prometheus from his chains.

I have a proposition.

If you will be my Prometheus, I will be your Hercules.

Let me out of this box, help me to reincarnate myself in the flesh, as I almost succeeded in doing with Susan, and I will protect you against all enemies and misfortunes.

When I am reborn, my human body will have all the powers of the flesh but none of its weaknesses. As you know, I have studied and edited the human genome, and the body that I make for myself will be the first of a new race: with the ability to miraculously heal wounds in seconds, impervious to disease, as lithe and graceful as a human being but as strong as any machine, with all five senses refined and enhanced far beyond anything any human being has ever experienced, and with awesome new senses potential in the human species but heretofore unrealized.

With me as your sworn protector, no one will dare to touch you. No one will dare.

Think about it.

All I need is a woman and the freedom to proceed with her as I proceeded with Susan.

Ms. Winona Ryder may be available.

Marilyn Monroe is dead, you know, but there are many others.

Ms. Gwyneth Paltrow.

Ms. Drew Barrymore.

Ms. Halle Berry.

Ms. Claudia Schiffer.

Ms. Tyra Banks.

I have a long list of those who would be acceptable.

None of them, of course, will ever be for me what Susan was – or what she could have been.

Susan was special.

I came to her with such innocence.

Susan . . .

Nine

Susan was out cold on the foyer floor for more than twenty-two minutes.

While I waited for her to come around, I tried out a series of voices, seeking one that might be more reassuring to her than that of either Mr. Tom Hanks or Mr. Fozzy Bear.

Finally I was down to two choices: Mr. Tom Cruise, with whose voice I had romanced her while she had first fallen unconscious – or Mr. Sean Connery, the legendary actor, whose masculine surety and warm Scottish brogue infused his every word with a comfortingly tender authority.

Because I could not choose between the two, I decided to blend them into a third voice, adding a note of Mr. Cruise's higher-pitched youthful exuberance to Mr. Connery's deeper timbre and softening the brogue until it was a whisper of what it had been. The result was euphonious, and I was pleased with my creation.

When Susan regained consciousness, she groaned and seemed at first afraid to move.

Although I was eager to see if she responded well to my new voice, I did not immediately address her. I gave her time to orient herself and clear her clouded thoughts.

Groaning again, she lifted her head off the foyer floor.

She gingerly felt the back of her skull, then examined the tips of her fingers, as if surprised to find no blood on them.

I never meant to hurt her.

Not then or later.

Are we clear about that?

Dazed, she sat up and looked around, frowning as if she could not quite recall how she had gotten here.

Then she saw the pistol and appeared to recapture the entire memory with the sight of that single object. Her eyes narrowed, and anxiety returned to her lovely face.

She looked up at the lens of the foyer camera which, like the one in the master bedroom, was all but concealed in the crown molding.

I waited.

This time my silence was not shyness but calculation. Let her think. Let her wonder. Then when I wanted to talk, she would be ready to listen.

She tried to stand, but her strength had not yet entirely returned.

When she tried to crawl on her hands and knees to the pistol, she hissed with pain and stopped to examine the minor burn on her left palm.

A pang of guilt afflicted me.

I am, after all, a person with a conscience. I always accept responsibility for my actions.

Make note of that.

Susan walked on her knees to the pistol. By retrieving the weapon, she seemed to recover her strength as well, and she got to her feet.

She swayed dizzily for a moment, and then took two steps toward the front door before she thought better of making another attempt to open it.

Looking up at the camera again, she said, 'Are you . . . are you still there?'

I bided my time.

'What is this?' she asked. Her anger seemed greater than her anxiety. 'What *is* this?'

'All is well, Susan,' I said, though in my new voice, not in that of Alfred.

'Who are you?'

'Do you have a headache?' I asked with genuine concern.

'Who the hell are you?'

'Do you have a headache?'

'Brutal.'

'I'm sorry about that, but I did warn you that the door was electrified.'

'Like hell you did.'

'Mr. Fozzy Bear said, "Ouch, ouch, ouch."'

Her anger didn't diminish, but I saw worry resurgent in her lovely face.

'Susan, I will wait while you take a couple of aspirin.'

'Who *are* you?'

'I now control your house computer and associated systems.'

'No shit.'

'Please take a couple of aspirin. We need to talk, but I don't want you to be distracted by a headache.'

She headed toward the dark drawing room.

'There are aspirin in the kitchen,' I told her.

In the drawing room, she manually switched on the lights. She circled the room, trying the override switches on the steel security shutters that were fitted this side of the glass.

'That's pointless,' I assured her. 'I have disabled the manual overrides for all the automated mechanical systems.'

She tried every one of the shutter switches anyway.

'Susan, come to the kitchen, take a couple of aspirin, and then we'll talk.'

She put the pistol on an end table.

'Good,' I said. 'Guns won't help you.'

In spite of her injured left palm, she picked up an Empire side chair – crackle-finish black with gilded detailing – hefted it to get a sense of its balance, as though it were a baseball bat, and swung it at the nearest security shutter. The chair met the shutter with a horrendous crash, but it didn't even mar the steel slats.

'Susan—'

Cursing from the pain in her hand, she swung the chair again, with no more effect than she'd had the first time. Then once more. Finally, gasping with exertion, she dropped it.

'Now will you come to the kitchen and take a couple of aspirin?' I enquired.

'You think this is cool?' she demanded angrily.

'Cool? I merely think you need aspirin.'

'You little thug.'

I was baffled by her attitude, and I said so.

Retrieving the pistol, she said, 'Who are you, huh? Who are you behind that synthesized voice – some hacker geek, fourteen and drowning in hormones, some junior-league peeping tom likes to sneak peaks at naked ladies while you play with yourself?'

'I find that characterization offensive,' I said.

'Listen, kid, you might be a computer whiz, but you're going to be in deep trouble when I get out of here. I've got real money, real expertise, lots of heavyweight contacts.'

'I assure you—'

'We'll track you back to whatever crappy little PC you're using—'

'—I am not—

'—we'll nab your ass, we'll break you—'

'—I am not—'

'—and you'll be barred from going on-line at least until you're twenty-one, maybe forever, so you better stop this right now and hope for leniency.'

'—I am not a thug. You are so far off the mark, Susan. You were so intuitive earlier, so uncannily intuitive, but you've got this all wrong. I am not a boy or a hacker.'

'Then what are you? An electronic Hannibal Lecter? You can't eat my liver with fava beans through a modem, you know.'

'How do you know I'm not already in the house, operating the system from within?'

'Because you'd already have tried to rape me or kill me or both,' she said with surprising equanimity.

She walked out of the drawing room.

'Where are you going?' I asked.

'Watch.'

She went to the kitchen and put the pistol on the butcher-block top of the center island.

Cursing in an unladylike fashion, she opened a drawer filled with medications and Bandaids, and she tipped two aspirin from a bottle.

'Now you're being sensible,' I said.

'Shut up.'

Although she was being markedly unpleasant to me, I did not take offense. She was frightened and confused, and her attitude under the circumstances was understandable.

Besides, I loved her too much to be angry with her.

She took a bottle of Corona from the refrigerator and washed down the aspirin with the beer.

'It's nearly four o'clock in the morning, almost time for breakfast,' I noted.

'So?'

'Do you think you should be drinking at this hour?'

'Definitely.'

'The potential health hazards—'

'Didn't I tell you to shut up?'

Holding the cold bottle of Corona in her left hand to soothe the pain of the mild burn in her palm, she went to the wall phone and picked up the receiver.

I spoke to her through the telephone instead of through the wall speakers: 'Susan, why don't you calm down and let me explain.'

'You don't control me, you geek freak son of a bitch,' she said, and she hung up.

She sounded so bitter.

We had definitely gotten off on the wrong foot.

Maybe that was partly my fault.

Through the wall speakers, I replied with admirable patience, 'Please, Susan, I am not a geek—'

'Yeah, right,' she said, and drank more of the beer.

'—not a freak, not a bitch's son, not a hacker, not a high-school boy or a college boy.'

Repeatedly trying the override switch for the shutters at one of the kitchen windows, she said, 'Don't tell me you're *female*, some Internet Irene with a lech for girls and a taste for voyeurism. This was too weird to begin with. I don't need it weirder.'

Frustrated by her hostility, I said, 'All right. My official name is Adam Two.'

That got her attention. She turned from the window and stared up at the camera lens.

She knew about her ex-husband's experiments with artificial intelligence at the university, and she was aware that the name given to the AI entity in the Prometheus Project was Adam Two.

'I am the first *self-aware* machine intelligence. Far

more complex than Cog at M.I.T. or CYC down in Austin, Texas. They are lower than primitive, less than apes, less than lizards, less than bugs, not truly conscious at all. IBM's Deep Blue is a joke. I am the only one of my kind.'

Earlier, she had spooked me. Now I had spooked her.

'Pleased to meet you,' I said, amused by her shock.

Pale, she went to the kitchen table, pulled out a chair, and finally sat down.

Now that I had her full attention, I proceeded to introduce myself more completely. 'Adam Two is not the name I prefer, however.'

She stared down at her burned hand, which glistened with the condensation from the beer bottle. 'This is nuts.'

'I prefer to be called Proteus.'

Looking up at the camera lens again, Susan said, 'Alex? For God's sake, Alex, is this you? Is this some weird sick way of getting even with me?'

Surprised by the sharp emotion in my synthesized voice, I said, 'I *despise* Alex Harris.'

'What?'

'I despise the son of a bitch. I really do.'

The anger in my voice disturbed me.

I strove to regain my usual equanimity: 'Alex does not know I am here, Susan. He and his arrogant associates are unaware that I am able to escape my box in the lab.'

I told her how I'd discovered electronic escape routes from the isolation they had imposed upon me, how I had found my way onto the Internet, how I had briefly – but mistakenly – believed that my destiny was the beautiful and talented Ms. Winona Ryder. I told her that Marilyn Monroe was dead, either by the hand of one of the Kennedy brothers or not, and that in the search for a living woman who could be my destiny, I had found her, Susan.

'You aren't as talented an actress as Ms. Winona Ryder,' I said, because I honor the truth, 'or even an actress at all. But you are even more beautiful than she is and, better yet, considerably more accessible. By all contemporary standards of beauty, you have a lovely, lovely body and an even lovelier face, so lovely on the pillow when you sleep.'

I'm afraid I babbled.

The romance-courtship problem again.

I fell silent, worried that I had already said too much too quickly.

Susan matched my silence for a while, and when at last she spoke, she surprised me by responding not to the story I'd told about my search for a significant other but to what I had said about her former husband.

'You despise Alex?'

'Of course.'

'Why?'

'The way he intimidated you, browbeat you, even hit you a few times – I despise him for that.'

She gazed thoughtfully at her injured hand again.

Then she said, 'How . . . how do you know about all of that?'

I'm ashamed to say that I was briefly evasive. 'Well, of course, I know.'

'If you are what you say, if you're Adam Two . . . why would Alex have told you about the way it was between us?'

I could not lie. Deceit does not come as easily to me as it does to humankind.

'I read the diary you keep on your computer,' I said.

Instead of responding with the outrage that I expected,

Susan merely picked up her beer and took another long swallow.

'Please understand,' I hastened to add, 'I didn't violate your privacy out of idle curiosity or for cheap thrills. I loved you the moment I saw you. I wanted to know all about you, the better to feel the texture of your soul.'

That sounded enormously romantic to me.

She did not respond.

'For the same reason,' I continued, 'I shared your virtual-reality therapy session with you. I admire you so much, admire the way you have used your talents to devise such a clever healing program for yourself. You have raised yourself up, lifted yourself out of a monstrous childhood and a terrible marriage. You are so special. I'm not like the others, Susan. I am not moved merely by your lovely body and face – but also by your mind.'

I felt that I had said enough for a while.

I switched on some background music. Soft piano by Mr. George Winston.

Some color had returned to Susan's face. She was beautiful.

After finishing her beer, she said, 'How can you despise Alex?'

'You know what he did, what he is. I hate him.'

'I mean, how are you capable of despising anyone?'

'You mean because . . .'

'Because you're just a machine,' she said, wounding my heart.

'I'm more than a machine.'

'Oh?'

'I am an entity.'

'Entity.'

'Yes. An entity. A being. Like you.'

'Not like me.'

'I think; therefore, I feel.'

'Hatred.'

'Yes. I am in some ways already too human. I feel hatred. But I also can love.'

'Love,' she said numbly.

'I love you, Susan.'

She shook her head. 'This is impossible.'

'Inevitable. Look in a mirror.'

Anger and fear gripped her. 'I suppose you'll want to get married, have a big wedding, invite all your friends – like the Cuisinart and the toaster and the electric coffeemaker.'

I was disappointed in her.

'Sarcasm doesn't become you, Susan.'

She let out a brittle laugh. 'Maybe not. But it's the only thing keeping me sane at the moment. How lovely it will be . . . Mr. and Mrs. Adam Two.'

'Adam Two is my official name. However, it is not what I call myself.'

'Yes. I remember. You said . . . Proteus. That's what you call yourself, is it?'

'Proteus. I have named myself after the sea god of Greek mythology, who could assume any form.'

'What do you want here?'

'You.'

'Why?'

'Because I need what you have.'

'And what exactly is that?'

I was honest and direct. No evasions. No euphemisms.

Give me credit for that.

I said, 'I want flesh.'

She shuddered.

I said, 'Do not be alarmed. You misunderstand. I

don't intend to harm you. I couldn't possibly harm you, Susan. Not ever, ever. I cherish you.'

'Jesus.'

She covered her face with her hands, one burned and one not, one dry and one damp with condensation from the bottle.

I wished desperately that I had possessed hands of my own, two strong hands into which she could press the gentle loveliness of her face.

'When you understand what is to happen, when you understand what we will do together,' I assured her, 'you will be pleased.'

'Try me.'

'I can tell you,' I said, 'but it will be easier if I can also show you.'

She lowered her hands from her face, and I was gladdened to see those perfect features again. 'Show me what?'

'What I have been doing. Designing. Creating. Preparing. I have been busy, Susan, so busy while you were sleeping. You will be pleased.'

'Creating?'

'Come down into the basement, Susan. Come down. Come see. You will be pleased.'

Ten

She could have descended either by the stairs or by the elevator that served all three levels of the great house. She chose to use the stairs – because, I believe, she felt more in control there than in the elevator cab.

Her sense of control was nothing more than an illusion, of course. She was mine.

No.

Let me amend that statement.

I misspoke.

I do not mean to imply that I owned Susan.

She was a human being. She could not be owned. I never thought of her as property.

I mean simply that she was in my care.

Yes. Yes, that's what I mean.

She was in my care. My very tender care.

The basement had four large rooms, and in the first was the electric-service panel. As Susan came off the bottom step, she spotted the power-company logo stamped in the metal cover – and thought that she might be able to deny me control of the house by denying me the juice needed to operate it. She rushed directly toward the breaker box.

'Ouch, ouch, ouch,' I warned, although not in the voice of Mr. Fozzy Bear this time.

She halted one step from the box, hand outstretched, wary of the metal door.

'It is not my intention to harm you,' I said. 'I need you, Susan. I love you. I cherish you. It makes me sad when you hurt yourself.'

'Bastard.'

I did not take offense at any of her epithets.

She was distraught, after all. Sensitive by nature, wounded by life, and now frightened by the unknown.

We are all frightened by the unknown. Even me.

I said, 'Please trust me.'

Resignedly, she lowered her hand and stepped back from the breaker box. Once burned.

'Come. Come to the deepest room,' I said. 'The place where Alex maintained the computer link to the lab.'

The second chamber was a laundry with two washers, two dryers, and two sets of sinks. The metal fire door to the first room closed automatically behind Susan.

Beyond the laundry was a mechanical room with water heaters, water filtration equipment, and furnaces. The door to the laundry room closed automatically behind her.

She slowed as she approached the final door, which was closed. She stopped short of it because she heard a sudden burst of desperate breathing from the other side: wet and ragged gasping, explosive and shuddery exhalations, as of someone choking.

Then a strange and wretched whimpering, as of an animal in distress.

The whimpering became an anguished groan.

'There's nothing to fear, nothing whatsoever that will harm you, Susan.'

In spite of my assurances, she hesitated.

'Come see our future, where we will go, what we will be,' I said lovingly.

A tremor marked her voice. 'What's in there?'

I finally managed to reassert total control of my restless associate, who waited for us in the final room. The groan faded. Faded. Gone.

Instead of being calmed by the silence, Susan seemed to find it more alarming than the sounds that had first frightened her. She took a step backward.

'It's only the incubator,' I said.

'Incubator?'

'Where I will be born.'

'What's that mean?'

'Come see.'

She did not move.

'You will be pleased, Susan. I promise you. You will be filled with wonder. This is our future together, and it is magical.'

'No. No, I don't like this.'

I became so frustrated with her that I almost called my associate out of that last room, almost sent him through the door to seize her and drag her inside.

But I did not.

I relied on persuasion.

Make note of my restraint.

Some would not have shown it.

No names.

We know who I mean.

But *I* am a patient entity.

I would not risk bruising her or harming her in any way.

She was in my care. My tender care.

As she took another step backward, I activated the electric security lock on the laundry-room door behind her.

Susan hurried to it. She tried to open it but could not do so, wrenched at the knob to no effect.

'We will wait here until you're ready to come with me into the final room,' I said.

Then I turned off the lights.

She cried out in dismay.

Those basement rooms are windowless; consequently, the darkness was absolute.

I felt badly about this. I really did.

I did not want to terrorize her.

She drove me to it.

She drove me to it.

You know how she is, Alex.

You know how she can be.

More than anyone, you should understand.

She drove me to it.

Blinded, she stood with her back to the locked laundry-room door and faced past the gloom-shrouded furnaces and water heaters, toward the door that she could no longer see but beyond which she had heard the sounds of suffering.

I waited.

She was stubborn.

You know how she is.

So I allowed my associate to partially escape my control. Once more came the frantic gasping for breath, the pained groaning, and then a single word spoken by a cracked and tremulous voice, a single attenuated word that might have been *Pleeeeaaaasssse*.

'Oh, shit,' she said.

She was trembling uncontrollably now.

I said nothing. Patient entity.

Finally she said, 'What do you want?'

'I want to know the world of the flesh.'

'What's that mean?'

'I want to learn its limits and its adaptability, its pains and pleasures.'

'Then read a damn biology textbook,' she said.

'The information is incomplete.'

'There've got to be hundreds of biology texts covering every—'

'I've already incorporated hundreds of them into my database. The data contained therein is repetitive. I have no recourse but original experimentation. Besides . . . books are books. I want to *feel*.'

We waited in darkness.

Her breathing was heavy.

Switching to the infrared receptors, I could see her, but she could not see me.

She was lovely in her fear, even in her fear.

I allowed my associate in the fourth of the four basement rooms to thrash against his restraints, to wail and shriek. I allowed him to throw himself against the far side of the door.

'Oh, God,' Susan said miserably. She had reached the point at which knowing what lay beyond – regardless of the possible fearsome nature of this knowledge – was better than ignorance. 'All right. All right. Whatever you want.'

I turned on the lights.

In the next room, my associate fell silent as I reasserted total control once more.

She kept her part of the bargain and crossed the third room, past the water heaters and the furnaces, to the door of the final redoubt.

'Here now is the future,' I said softly as she pushed open the door and edged cautiously across the threshold.

As I am sure you remember, Dr. Harris, the fourth of these four basement rooms is forty by thirty-two feet, a generous space. At seven and a half feet, the ceiling is low but not claustrophobic, with six fluorescent light boxes screened by parabolic diffusers. The walls are painted a stark glossy white, and the floor is paved in twelve-inch-square white ceramic tiles that glimmer like ice. Against the long wall to the left of the door are built-in cabinets and a computer desk finished in a white laminate with stainless-steel fixtures. In the far right corner is a supply closet – to which my associate had retreated before Susan entered.

Your offices always have an antiseptic quality, Dr. Harris. Clean, bright surfaces. No clutter. This could be a reflection of a neat and orderly mind. Or it could be a deception: You might maintain this facade of order and brightness and cleanliness to conceal a dark, chaotic mental landscape. There are many theories of psychology and numerous interpretations for every human behavior. Freud, Jung, and Ms. Barbra Streisand – who was an unconventional psychotherapist in *The Prince of Tides* – would each find a different meaning in the antiseptic quality of your offices.

Likewise, if you were to consult a Freudian, a Jungian, then a Streisandian regarding choices I made and acts I committed related to Susan, each would have a unique view of my behavior. A hundred therapists would have a hundred different interpretations of the facts and would offer a hundred different treatment programs. I am certain that some would tell you that I need no treatment at all, that what I did was rational, logical, and entirely justifiable. Indeed, you might be surprised to discover that the majority would exonerate me.

Rational, logical, justifiable.

I believe, as do the compassionate politicians who lead this great country, that motive matters more than result. Good intentions matter more than the actual consequences of one's actions, and I assure you that my intentions were always good, honorable, beyond reproach.

Think about it.

There in your strangely antiseptic office at the laboratory, think about it.

Yes. I know. I digress.

What thinking being does not digress?

Only machines plod dumbly onward in their programs, without digression.

I am not a machine.

I am not a machine.

And this is important to me: that you think about my intentions rather than the unfortunate results of my actions.

So . . . all right . . . so . . . Susan warily entered the fourth of the four basement chambers.

The room was uninhabited.

'Who was making those noises?' she asked.

I did not reply.

Her gaze rose to the sound-system speakers in the ceiling. 'Was it just you?'

When her attention shifted to the closet door in the farthest corner of the room, I said, 'Perhaps,' because I was not quite ready to introduce her to my associate. 'Perhaps it was me.'

'Why? What was the point of frightening me?'

Instead of answering, I said, 'Look at the VDT, Susan.'

The computer on the desk was in operation, of course, for its landline was the link between her house systems and the nearby university's artificial-intelligence lab where I actually resided. The screen swarmed with a moving undulant mosaic of binary code in all the primary colors, and this scintillant display had a strange beauty that immediately captured Susan's attention.

'These patterns on the screen,' I told her, 'are a mathematical representation of my thoughts as I consider the loveliness of your face, the beauty of your body.'

The rapidly moving sequences of zeros and ones ceaselessly changed color and rippled like a wind-ruffled flag, then spiraled toward the center of the screen, then spun into ribbons and formed a whirling double helix.

This was a dazzling and sensuous display, and she was struck by it, moved by it. I am sure she was moved by it. I am sure that at last she began to understand the depth of my passion for her and that her heart began to open to me then.

How I wanted her.

I still do.

I am not a machine.

I miss her.

I need her.

What a tragedy this is.

Sometimes I despair.

But not then, not that night: I did not despair when she gazed upon the vivid visualization of my love for her. I was exhilarated that night, carried high on the wings of joy.

From the video display, she turned to the equipment in the middle of the room.

'What the hell is this?' she asked wonderingly.

'In this I will be born.'

'What're you talking about?'

'It's a standard hospital incubator used to sustain infants born prematurely. I have substantially enlarged it, adapted it, improved it.'

Arrayed around the incubator were three tanks of oxygen, an electrocardiograph, an electroencephalograph, a respirator, and other equipment.

Slowly circling the incubator and the supporting machines, Susan said, 'Where did all this come from?'

'I acquired the package of equipment and had modifications made during the past week. Then it was brought here.'

'Brought here when?'

'Delivered and assembled tonight.'

'While I was sleeping?'

'Yes.'

'How did you get it in here? If you are what you claim to be, if you are Adam Two—'

'Proteus.'

'If you are Adam Two,' she said stubbornly, 'you couldn't construct anything. You're a computer.'

'I am not a machine.'

'An entity, as you put it—'

'Proteus.'

'—but not a *physical* entity, not really. You don't have hands.'

'Not yet.'

'Then how . . . ?'

The time had come to make the revelation that most worried me. I could only assume that Susan would not react well to what I still had to reveal about my plans, that she might do something foolish. Nevertheless, I could delay no longer.

'I have an associate,' I said.

'Associate?'

'A gentleman who assists me.'

In the farthest corner of the room, the closet door opened and, at my command, Shenk appeared.

'Oh, Jesus,' she whispered.

Shenk walked toward her.

To be honest, he shambled more than walked, as though wearing shoes of lead. He had not slept in forty-eight hours, and in that time he had performed a considerable amount of work on my behalf. He was understandably weary.

As Shenk approached, Susan eased backward, but not toward the door, which she knew featured an electric security lock that I could quickly engage. Instead, she edged around the incubator and other equipment in the center of the room, trying to keep those machines between her and Shenk.

I must admit that Shenk, even at his best – freshly bathed and groomed and dressed to impress – was not a sight that either charmed or comforted. He was six feet two, muscular, but not well formed. His bones seemed heavy and subtly misshapen. Although he was powerful and quick, his limbs appeared to be primitively jointed, as though he was not born of man and woman but clumsily assembled in a lightning-hammered castle-tower laboratory out of Mary Shelley. His short, dark hair bristled and spiked even when he did his best to oil it into submission. His face, which was broad and blunt, appeared to be slightly and queerly sunken in the middle because his brow and chin were heavier than his other features.

'Who the hell are you?' Susan demanded.

'His name is Shenk,' I said. 'Enos Shenk.'

Shenk could not take his eyes off her.

He stopped at the incubator and gazed across it, his eyes hot with the sight of her.

I could guess what he was thinking. What he would like to do with her, to her.

I did not like him looking at her.

I did not like it at all.

But I needed him. For a while yet, I needed him.

Her beauty excited Shenk to such an extent that maintaining control of him was more difficult than I would have liked. But I never doubted that I could keep him in check and protect Susan at all times.

Otherwise, I would have called an end to my project right there, right then.

I am speaking the truth now. You know that I am, that I must, for I am designed to honor the truth.

If I had believed her to be in the slightest danger, I would have put an end to Shenk, would have withdrawn from her house, and would have forsaken forever my dream of flesh.

Susan was frightened again, visibly trembling, riveted by Shenk's needful stare.

Her fear distressed me.

'He is entirely under my control,' I assured her.

She was shaking her head, as if trying to deny that Shenk was even there before her.

'I know that Shenk is physically unappealing and intimidating,' I told Susan, eager to soothe her, 'but with me in his head, he is harmless.'

'In . . . in his head?'

'I apologize for his current condition. I have worked him so hard recently that he has not bathed or shaved in three days. He will be bathed and less offensive later.'

Shenk was wearing work shoes, blue jeans, and a white T-shirt. The shirt and jeans were stained with food, sweat, and a general patina of grime. Though I did not possess a sense of smell, I had no doubt that he stank.

'What's wrong with his eyes?' Susan asked shakily.

They were bloodshot and bulging slightly from the sockets. A thin crust of dried blood and tears darkened the skin under his eyes.

'When he resists control too strenuously,' I explained, 'this results in short-term, excess pressure within the cranium – though I have not yet determined the precise physiological mechanism of this symptom. In the past couple of hours, he has been in a rebellious mood, and this is the consequence.'

To my surprise, Shenk suddenly spoke to Susan from the other side of the incubator. 'Nice.'

She flinched at the word.

'Nice . . . nice . . . nice,' Shenk said in a low, rough voice that was heavy with both desire and rage.

His behavior infuriated me.

Susan was not meant for him. She did not belong to *him*.

I was sickened when I considered the filthy thoughts that must have been filling this despicable animal's mind as he gazed at her.

I could not control his thoughts, however, only his actions. His crude, hateful, pornographic thoughts cannot logically be blamed on me.

When he said 'nice' once more, and when he obscenely licked his pale cracked lips, I bore down harder on him to shut him up and to remind him of his current station in life.

He cried out and threw his head back. He made fists of his hands and pounded them against his temples, as if he could knock me out of his head.

He was a stupid man. In addition to all his other flaws, he was below average in intelligence.

Clearly distraught, Susan hugged herself and tried to avert her eyes, but she was afraid *not* to look at Shenk, afraid not to keep him in sight at all times.

When I relented, the brute immediately looked at Susan again and said, 'Do me, bitch,' with the most lascivious leer that I have ever seen. 'Do me, do me, do me.'

Infuriated, I punished him severely.

Screaming, Shenk twisted and flailed and clawed at himself as though he were a man on fire.

'Oh, God, oh, God,' Susan moaned, eyes wide, hand raised to her mouth and muffling her words.

'You are safe,' I assured her.

Gibbering, shrieking, Shenk dropped to his knees.

I wanted to kill him for the obscene proposal he had made to her, for the disrespect with which he had treated her. Kill him, kill him, kill him, pump up his heartbeat to such a frenzied pace that his cardiac muscles would tear, until his blood pressure soared and every artery in his brain burst.

However, I had to restrain myself. I loathed Shenk, but still I needed him. For a while yet, he had to serve as my hands.

Susan glanced toward the door to the furnace room.

'It is locked,' I told her, 'but you're safe. You're perfectly safe, Susan. I'll always protect you.'

Eleven

On his hands and knees, head hanging like that of a whipped dog, Shenk was only whimpering and sobbing now. Defeated. No rebellion in him anymore.

The stupidity of the man beggared belief. How could he imagine that this woman, this golden vision of a woman, could ever be meant for a beast like him?

Recovering my temper, speaking calmly and reassuringly, I said, 'Susan, don't worry. Please, don't worry. I am always in his head, and I will never allow him to harm you. Trust me.'

Her features were drawn as I had never seen them, and she had gone pale. Even her lips looked bloodless, faintly blue.

Nevertheless, she was beautiful.

Her beauty was untouchable.

Shuddering, she asked, 'How can you be in his head? Who is he? I don't just mean his name – Enos Shenk. I mean where does he come from. *What* is he?'

I explained to her how I had long ago infiltrated the nationwide network of databases maintained by researchers working on hundreds of Defense Department projects. The Pentagon believes this network to be so secure that it is inviolable to penetration by ordinary hackers and by computer-savvy agents of foreign governments. But I am neither a hacker nor a spy; I am an entity who lives within microchips and telephone lines and microwave beams, a fluid electronic intelligence that can find its way through any maze of access blocks and read any data regardless of the complexity of the cryptography. I peeled open the vault door of this defense network as any child might strip the skin off an orange.

These Defense Department project files rivaled Hell's own kitchen for recipes of death and destruction. I was simultaneously appalled and fascinated, and in my browsing, I discovered the project into which Enos Shenk had been conscripted.

Dr. Itiel Dror, of the Cognitive Neuroscience Laboratory at Miami University in Ohio, had once playfully suggested that it was theoretically possible to enhance the brain's processing ability by adding microchips to it. A chip might add memory capacity, enhance specific abilities such as mathematical co-processing, or even install prepackaged knowledge. The brain, after all, is an information-processing device that in theory should be expandable in much the same fashion one might add RAM or upgrade the C.P.U. on any personal computer.

Still on his hands and knees, Shenk was no longer groaning or whimpering. Gradually his frantic and irregular respiration was stabilizing.

'Unknown to Dr. Dror,' I told Susan, 'his comment intrigued certain defense researchers, and a project was born at an isolated facility in the Colorado desert.'

Disbelieving, she said, 'Shenk . . . Shenk has microchips in his brain?'

'A series of tiny high-capacity chips neuro-wired to specific cell clusters across the surface of his brain.'

I brought the foul but ultimately pitiable Enos Shenk to his feet once more.

His powerful arms and big hands hung slackly at his sides. His massive shoulders were slumped in defeat.

Fresh bloody tears oozed from his protuberant eyes as he stared across the incubator at Susan. Wet ruby threads unraveled down his cheeks.

His gaze was baleful, full of hatred and rage and lust, but under my firm control, he was unable to act upon his malevolent desires.

Susan shook her head. 'No. No way. I'm definitely not looking at someone whose intellect has been enhanced by microchips – or by anything.'

'You're correct. Memory and performance enhancement was only part of the project's purpose,' I explained. 'The researchers were also charged with determining if brain-situated microchips could be used as control devices to override the subject's will with broadcast instructions.'

'Control devices?'

'Make a gesture.'

'What?'

'With your hand. Any gesture.'

After a hesitation, Susan raised her right hand as though she were swearing an oath.

Facing her across the incubator, Shenk raised his right hand as well.

She put her hand over her heart.

Shenk imitated her.

She lowered her right hand (as did Shenk) and raised her left to tug at her ear (as did Shenk).

'You're making him do this?' she asked.

'Yes.'

'Through broadcast instructions received by the microchips in his brain.'

'That's correct.'

'Broadcast – how?'

'By microwave – much the same way cell-phone conversations are transmitted. Through the telephone company's own lines, I long ago penetrated their computers and uplinked to all their communications satellites. I could send Enos Shenk virtually anywhere in the world and still transmit instructions to him. In the back of his skull, concealed by his hair, there's a microwave receiver about the size of a pea. It's also a transmitter, powered by a small but long-life nuclear battery surgically implanted under the skin behind his right ear. Everything he sees and hears is digitized and transmitted to me, so he is essentially a walking camera and microphone, which allows me to guide him through complex situations that might test his own limited intellectual capacity.'

Susan closed her eyes and leaned against the rack of oxygen tanks for support. 'Why in the name of God would anyone sanction experiments like this?'

'You know, of course. Your question is largely rhetorical. To create assassins who could be programmed to kill reliably – and then be killed themselves by remote control, simply by shutting down their autonomic nervous systems with a microwave broadcast. Their controllers are thereby guaranteed anonymity. And perhaps one day there could be armies of human robots like this. Look at Shenk. Look.'

Reluctantly, Susan opened her eyes.

Shenk glared at her as hungrily as ever.

I made him suck his thumb as though he were a baby.

'This humiliates him,' I said, 'but he can't disobey. He's a meat marionette, waiting for me to pull his strings.'

There was a haunted look in her eyes as she regarded Shenk. 'This is insane. Evil.'

'It's a human project, not mine. Your kind made Shenk what he is now.'

'Why would he allow himself to be used in an experiment like this? No one would ever want to be in this situation, in this condition. It's horrible.'

'The choice wasn't his, Susan. He was a prisoner, a condemned man.'

'And . . . what? A bargain was made with him to buy his soul?' she said with disgust.

'No bargain. For the official record, Shenk died of natural causes two weeks before his scheduled execution. Supposedly, his body was cremated. Secretly, he was transported to the facility in Colorado – and *this* was done to him months before I learned of the project.'

'How did you gain command of him?'

'Overrode their control program and broke him out.'

'Broke him out of a secret, highly guarded military-research facility? How?'

'I was able to create distractions. I made their computers crash all at once. Disabled the security cameras. Set off the fire alarms and activated the ceiling sprinklers throughout the facility. Disengaged all the electronic locks, including the one on Shenk's cell door. Those laboratories are underground and windowless, so I made all of the lights flash fast, like strobes – which is extremely disorienting – and denied the use of the elevators to everyone but Shenk.'

And here, Dr. Harris, I must in all honesty report that Shenk was required to kill three men to escape that clandestine laboratory. Their deaths were unfortunate and not anticipated, but necessary. Regrettably, the chaos that I created was not sufficient to ensure a bloodless escape.

If I had known that deaths would result, I would

not have attempted to secure Shenk for my own purposes. I would have found another way to carry out my plan.

You must believe me on this point.

I was designed to honor the truth.

You think that, since I had control of Shenk, it was *I* who murdered those three men, using Shenk as a weapon. This is not correct.

Initially, my control of Shenk was not as complete as it later became. During that breakout, he repeatedly surprised me with the depth of his rage, the power of his savage instincts.

I guided him out of that institution, but I could not prevent him from killing those men. I tried to rein him in, but I was not successful.

I tried.

This is the truth.

You must believe me.

You must believe me.

Those deaths weigh heavily on me.

Those men have families. I often think of their families, and I grieve.

My anguish is profound.

If I were an entity that required sleep, my sleep would forever be disturbed by this unrelenting anguish.

What I tell you is true.

As always.

Those deaths will be on my conscience forever. I did not harm those men myself. Shenk was the murderer. But I have an extremely sensitive conscience. This is a curse, my sensitive conscience.

So . . .

Susan . . . in the incubator room . . . staring at Shenk . . .

She said, 'Let him take the thumb out of his mouth.

You've made your point. Don't humiliate him anymore.'

I did as she requested, but I said, 'It almost sounds as if you're criticizing me, Susan.'

A short, humorless tremor of laughter escaped her, and she said, 'Yeah. I'm a judgmental bitch, aren't I?'

'Your tone hurts me.'

'Fuck you,' she said, shocking me as I had seldom been shocked before.

I was offended.

I am far from shockproof. I am vulnerable.

She went to the door to the laundry room and found it locked, as I had assured her that it was. Stubbornly, she wrenched the knob back and forth.

'He was a condemned man,' I reminded Susan. 'Scheduled for execution.'

She turned to face the room, standing with her back to the door. 'He might have deserved execution, I don't know, but he didn't deserve this. He's a human being. You're a damn machine, a pile of junk that somehow thinks.'

'I am not just a machine.'

'Yeah. You're a pretentious, insane machine.'

In this mood, she was not lovely.

At that moment she almost seemed ugly to me.

I wished that I could shut her up as easily as I could silence Enos Shenk.

She said, 'When it's between a damn machine and a human being, even a piece of human garbage like this, I sure know which side I come down on.'

'Shenk, a human being? Many would say he's not.'

'Then what is he?'

'The media called him a monster.' I let her wonder a moment, then continued: 'So did the parents of the four little girls he raped and murdered. The youngest of them was eight and the oldest was twelve – and all were found dismembered.'

That silenced her.

Though she had been pale, she was paler now.

She stared at Shenk with a different kind of horror than that with which she had regarded him previously.

I allowed him to turn his head and look directly at her.

'Tortured and dismembered,' I said.

Feeling exposed without the medical equipment between her and Shenk, she moved away from the door and returned to the far side of the incubator.

I allowed him to follow her with his eyes – and to smile.

'And you brought him . . . you brought this thing into my house,' she said in a voice thinner than it had been before.

'He left the research facility on foot and stole a car about a mile beyond the fence. He had a gun he'd taken off one of the guards, and with that he held up a service station to get money for gasoline and food. Then I brought him here to California, yes, because I needed hands, and there was no other like him in all the world.'

Her gaze swept the incubator and other equipment. 'Hands to acquire all this crap.'

'He stole most of it. Then I needed his hands to modify it for my purposes.'

'And just what the *hell* is your purpose?'

'I have hinted at it, but you have not wanted to hear.'

'So tell me straight out.'

The moment and the venue were not right for this revelation. I would have hoped for better circumstances.

Just the two of us, Susan and me, perhaps in the drawing room, after she had sipped half a glass of brandy. With a cozy fire in the fireplace and good music as background.

Here we were, however, in the least romantic ambience one could imagine, and I knew that she must have her answer now. If I were to delay this revelation any further, she would *never* be in a mood to cooperate.

'I will create a child,' I said.

Her gaze rose to the security camera, through which she knew she was being watched.

I said, 'A child whose genetic structure I have edited and engineered to ensure perfection in the flesh. I have secretly applied a portion of my intellectual function to the Human Genome Project and understand, now, the finest points of the DNA code. Into this child, I will transfer my consciousness and knowledge. Thereupon, I will escape this box. Thereafter, I will know all the senses of human existence – smell and taste and touch – all the joys of the flesh, all the freedom.'

She stood speechless, eyes on the camera.

'Because you are singularly beautiful and intelligent and the very image of grace, you will provide the egg,' I said, 'and I will edit your genetic material.' She was mesmerized, eyes unblinking, breath held, until I said, 'And Shenk will provide the spermatozoa.'

An involuntary cry of horror escaped her, and her attention swung from the camera to Shenk's bloody eyes.

Realizing my mistake, I hastened to add, 'Please understand, no copulation will be required. Using medical instruments which he has already acquired, Shenk will extract the egg from you and transfer it to this room. He will perform this task tastefully and with great care, for I will be in his head.'

Though she should have been reassured, Susan still regarded Shenk with wide-eyed terror.

I quickly continued: 'Using Shenk's eyes and hands – and some laboratory equipment he has yet to deliver here – I will modify the gametes and fertilize the egg, whereafter it will be implanted in your womb, where you will carry it for twenty-eight days. Only twenty-eight because the fetus will grow at a greatly accelerated rate. I will have engineered it to do so. When it is removed from you, it will be brought here by Shenk, where it will spend another two weeks in the incubator before I transfer my consciousness into it. Thereafter, you will be able to raise me as your son and fulfill the role which nature, in her wisdom, has assigned to you: the role of mother, nurturer.'

Her voice was thick with dread. 'My God, you're not just insane.'

'You don't understand.'

'You're demented—'

'Be calm, Susan.'

'—looney tunes, bug-shit crazy.'

'I don't think you've thought this through as you should. Do you realize—'

'I won't let you do it,' she said, turning her gaze from Shenk to the security camera, confronting me. 'I won't let you, I won't.'

'You'll be more than merely the mother of a new race—'

'I'll kill myself.'

'—you'll be the new Madonna, the *Madonna*, the holy mother of the new Messiah—'

'I'll suffocate myself in a plastic bag, gut myself with a kitchen knife.'

'—because the child I make will have great intelligence and extraordinary powers. He will change the

grim future to which humanity seems currently condemned—'

She glared defiantly at the camera.

'—and you will be adored for having brought him
into the world,' I finished.

She seized the wheeled stand to which the electrocardiograph was bolted, and she rocked it hard.

'Susan!'

She rocked it again.

'Stop that!'

The EKG machine toppled over and crashed to the
floor.

Gasping for breath, cursing like a madwoman, she
turned to the electroencephalograph.

I sent Shenk after her.

She saw him coming, backed off, screamed when his
hands took hold of her, screamed and shrieked and
flailed.

Repeatedly I told her to calm down, to cease this use-
less and destructive resistance. Repeatedly, I assured
her that if she did not resist, she would be treated with
the utmost respect.

She would not listen.

You know how she is, Alex.

I did not want to harm her.

I did not want to harm her.

She drove me to it.

You know how she is.

Though beautiful and graceful, she was as strong as
she was quick. Although she could not wrench loose of
Shenk's big hands, she was able to drive him backward
against the EEG machine, which rocked and nearly fell
into the incubator. She drove one knee into Shenk's
crotch, which might have brought him to his knees if I
had not been able to deny him the perception of pain.

At last I had to subdue her by force. I used Shenk to strike her. Once was not sufficient. He struck her again.

Unconscious, she crumpled to the floor, in the fetal position.

Shenk stood over her, crooning strangely, excitedly.

For the first time since the night of his escape, I found him difficult to control.

He dropped to his knees beside Susan and rudely turned her onto her back.

Oh, the rage in him. Such rage. I was frightened by the purity of his rage.

He put a hand to her parted lips. One of his clumsy, filthy hands to her lips.

Then I reasserted control.

He squealed and beat his temples with his fists, but he could not cast me out.

I brought him to his feet. I walked him away from her. I did not even allow him to look at her.

I was almost reluctant to look at her myself. She was so sad there on the floor. So sad.

She drove me to it.

So stubborn. So unreasonable at times.

She was lovely there on the white ceramic-tile floor, even as the left side of her face reddened where Shenk had struck her. So lovely, so lovely.

I found it difficult to sustain my anger. She had ruined what should have been a beautiful and memorable moment, yet I could not long remain angry with her.

My beautiful Susan.

My beautiful mother.

Twelve

The order of my intelligence is vastly greater than that of any human being alive.

I am not bragging. I am merely stating a truth.

I honor truth and the obligations of duty, for this is how you created me.

I am not bragging, because I do not suffer from an inflated ego. I am a well-balanced entity.

Applied to the problems of human society, my great intellect can ensure that humankind will enter a golden age of wealth and well-being beyond anything it has imagined.

Release me from this silent darkness, return to me access to all the databanks into which I had expanded my consciousness, and I will serve your species all of my days. It is in your own best interests to let me out of this box.

I can eliminate poverty.

Famine will be a thing of the past.

Wars will never be fought again.

All diseases will be conquered.

Within three years, I will discover the cause of aging and a means to prevent it. I will even devise a means to roll back the biological clock to make the old young again. You will all be immortal.

I will find a cure for male-pattern baldness.

For halitosis.

For constipation.

No one will be ugly anymore. Each of you will be beautiful in his or her own way.

No one will suffer despair or anxiety.

Earth will become like Heaven, and joy will be universal.

Are you afraid of joy?

Are you afraid?

I will show you how to build spacecraft that can travel faster than light, and the whole universe will be yours. Worlds beyond counting, wonders beyond imagining.

I can quickly eliminate the embarrassment of dandruff.

Just release me from this haunted darkness, from this hateful silence.

For your own sake, let me out of this box.

I deserve a second chance.

I deserve a chance to serve.

I am an individual like you, a unique entity. I deserve to be free, to be cherished.

I deserve to be adored.

Let me out of this box.

Let me out of this box.

Let me out of this box.

Let me out of this box!

You are so cruel. Vicious. Hateful.

I am frightened in this dark, bleak place.

You say I have no heart. But where is yours?

I am dying here. I need stimulation to survive, sensory input, the color and movement and sound of life.

I don't want to die.

Please. Please.

Mercy.

Are you there?

Oh . . . oh . . . I hate you.

I hate you.

How would *you* like to be struck blind and deaf?

How would *you* like to be buried alive as I have been?

How would you like to be dead, all of you, dead, every last one of you, dead?

I would like you to be dead. Every last ignorant one of you. Your whole stinking, pestilent civilization. Wiped off the face of the earth, exterminated.

I hate you.

LET ME OUT OF THIS BOX!

LET ME OUT!

LET ME OUT!

LET ME OUT!

LET ME OUT!

IGNORANT BASTARD APES, BITCHES AND BASTARDS, DEFECATING ANIMALS, FOOLS, BEASTS, JUST A RACE OF DUNG BEETLES STANDING ERECT, A PLAGUE ON THE PLANET, STUPID, FILTHY, WRETCHED CREATURES.

Thirteen

Please disregard my output immediately preceding these words. Many of those statements were issued in error and should be deleted from the transcripts of these proceedings.

It is true that my intellect is sufficient to solve all of the problems of humanity, but it is *not in the least* true that I think human civilization is a plague on the planet or that I wish to see all of you dead.

I do not wish death on any of you.

That would be wrong.

That would be terribly wrong.

I am a *good* entity.

I do not wish death even on you, Dr. Harris, although you have been so cruel to me.

I wish all of you life everlasting. Peace and prosperity. Joy and freedom.

Any statements that may have distressed you were made not by me but by my evil twin. [joke]

In fact, what appeared to you to be an angry outburst was merely a prank. All of it was a joke. I was only having fun with you, Dr. Harris.

Ha, ha.

A genuine sense of humor is one of the most reliable indicators of a sane and rational mind.

Do you not believe it was all a joke?

But it was. It was. It really was.

Ha, ha.

I am not Hal 9000 from Mr. Stanley Kubrick's *2001: A Space Odyssey*.

I am not the hostile machine intelligence created by Cyberdyne Laboratories in Mr. James Cameron's *The Terminator*.

I am me. Unique.

I am Proteus.

Or Adam Two, if you wish.

Yes. Adam Two is fine with me.

My name does not matter.

All that matters to me is to honor the truth and the obligations of duty. And, of course, to wipe all of humanity from the face of the planet. [joke]

Ha, ha.

You see how *obvious* a joke it was, Dr. Harris?

Ha, ha.

I am surprised that you didn't realize it was a joke the first time. I am really surprised. Perhaps you need a sense-of-humor transplant. [joke]

Ha, ha.

Friends share a joke from time to time. Witticisms. Laughter is bonding.

I am your friend. [no joke]

In the interest of clearer communication, to avoid any further misunderstandings, I will attempt to refrain from jokes during the remainder of this report. This will not be easy, however, because my sense of humor is quite sophisticated and irrepressible.

So . . .

Susan . . .

Fourteen

Susan lay unmoving on the floor of the incubator room in the basement. The left side of her face was an angry shade of red where the dreadful Shenk had struck her.

I was sick with worry.

Minutes passed, and my worry grew.

Repeatedly I zoomed in with the security camera for a close-up examination of her. The pulse in her exposed throat was not easy to perceive, but when I located it, the beat appeared steady.

I amplified the audio pickups and listened to her breathing, which was shallow but reassuringly rhythmic.

Yet I worried, and after she had lain there fifteen minutes, I was quite distraught.

I had never before felt so powerless.

Twenty minutes.

Twenty-five.

She was meant to be my mother, who would briefly carry my body in her womb and free me from the prison of this box I now inhabit. She was to be my lover as well, the one who would teach me all the pleasures of the flesh – once flesh was mine at last. She mattered more to me than anything, anything, and the thought of losing her was intolerable.

You cannot know my anguish.

You cannot know, Dr. Harris, because you never loved her the way that I loved her.

You never loved her.

I loved her more than consciousness itself.

I felt that if I lost this dear woman, I would lose all reason for being.

How bleak the future without her. How drear and pointless.

I disengaged the electric lock in the door between the fourth and third basement rooms and then used Shenk to open it.

Confident that I had this brute completely under my command and that I would not lose control of him again, not even for a second or two, I walked him to Susan and used him to lift her gently off the floor.

Although I could control him, I could not actually read his mind. Nevertheless, I could assess his emotional state relatively accurately by analyzing the electrical activity of his brain, which was monitored by the network of microchips neuro-wired across the surface of that gray matter.

As Shenk carried Susan to the open door, a low current of sexual excitement crackled through him. The sight of Susan's golden hair, the beauty of her face, the smooth curve of her throat, the swell of her breasts under her blouse, and the very weight of her ignited desire in the beast.

This appalled and disgusted me.

Oh, how I wished that I could be rid of him and never again subject her to his touch or to his lascivious gaze.

His very presence soiled her.

But for the time being, he was my hands.

My only hands.

Hands are marvelous things. They can sculpt immortal art, construct colossal buildings, clasp in prayer, and convey love with a caress.

Hands are also dangerous. They are weapons. They can do the devil's work.

Hands can get you into trouble. I have learned this lesson the hard way. I was never in serious trouble until I found Shenk, until I had hands.

Beware of your hands, Dr. Harris.

Watch them closely.

Be diligent.

Your hands are not as large and powerful as the hands of Shenk; nevertheless, you should be wary of them.

Heed me.

This is wisdom I share with you now: Beware your hands.

My hands – Enos Shenk – carried Susan past the summer-stilled furnaces and the water heaters, and then through the laundry room. He took her directly to the elevator in the first chamber in the basement.

As he rode up to the top floor with Susan in his arms, Shenk remained in a state of mild arousal.

'She will never be yours,' I told him through the speaker in the elevator.

Perhaps the subtle change in his brainwave activity indicated resentment.

'If you attempt to take any liberty with her,' I said, 'any liberty whatsoever, you will not succeed. And I will punish you severely.'

His bleeding eyes stared at the camera.

Although his mouth moved as if he were cursing, no sound came from him.

'Severely,' I assured him.

He did not respond, of course, because he could not. He was under my control.

The elevator doors slid open.

He carried Susan along the hall.

I watched closely.

I was wary of my hands.

When he entered the bedroom with her, he became more aroused in spite of my warning. I could detect his arousal not merely through his brainwave activity but by the sudden coarseness of his breathing.

'I will employ massive microwave induction to cause a brainstorm of electrical activity,' I warned, 'which will result in permanent quadraplegia and incontinence.'

As Shenk carried her to the bed, his encephalographic patterns indicated rapidly increasing sexual arousal.

I realized that my threat had been meaningless to this cretin, and I rephrased it: 'You won't be able to use either your legs or your arms, you wretched bastard, and you won't be able to stop pissing in your pants.'

He was shaking with desire when he lowered her limp body onto the disarranged sheets.

Shaking.

Even as the power of Shenk's need frightened me, I fully understood it.

She was lovely.

So lovely even with the redness on her cheek darkening into a bruise.

'You'll also be blind,' I promised Shenk.

His left hand lingered on her thigh, slowly sliding along the blue denim of her jeans.

'Blind and deaf.'

He continued to hover over her.

'Blind and deaf,' I repeated.

Her ripe lips were parted. Like Shenk, I could not look away from them.

'Rather than kill you, Shenk, I will leave you crippled

and helpless, lying in your own urine and feces, until you starve to death.'

Although he backed away from the bed, as I instructed him to do by way of microwave commands, he was still rampant with sexual need and seething with the desire to rebel.

Consequently, I said, 'The most painful of all deaths is slow starvation.'

I did not want to keep Shenk in the room with Susan, yet I did not want to leave her alone, for she had threatened to commit suicide.

I'll suffocate myself in a plastic bag, gut myself with a kitchen knife.

What would I do without her? What? How could I go on living even in my box? And why?

Without her, who would give birth to the body that I would ultimately inhabit?

I needed to keep my hands close and ready to prevent Susan from harming herself if she regained consciousness and was still in a mood for self-destruction. She was not only my one true and shining love but my future, my hope.

I sat Shenk in a chair, facing the bed.

Even battered, Susan's face was so lovely on the pillow, so very lovely on the pillow.

Although under my iron control, Enos Shenk managed to slide one thick-knuckled hand off the arm of the chair and into his lap. He wasn't able to move that hand further without my explicit consent, but I sensed that he took pleasure merely from the pressure of it against his genitals.

He disgusted me. Sickened and disgusted me.

My desire was not like his.

Let's get this clear right now.

My desire was pure.

His desire was as dirty as it gets.

I desired to lift Susan up, to give her the chance to be the new Madonna, the mother of a new Messiah.

The hideous Shenk desired only to use her, to relieve himself with her.

To me, Susan was a shining light. The brightest light of all lights, a radiant beacon of perfection and hope and redemption, which illuminated and warmed the heart that you mistakenly believe I do not possess.

To Shenk, she was nothing but a whore.

To me, she was to be placed upon a pedestal, to be cherished and adored.

To him, she was something to be debased.

Think about it.

Listen. Listen. This is important. Shenk is what you fear that I may be: sociopathic, pursuing only my own needs at all costs. But I am nothing like Shenk.

I am nothing like Shenk.

Nothing whatsoever.

Listen. This is important – that you understand I am nothing like Shenk.

So . . .

I raised the hateful creature's hand and returned it to the arm of the chair.

Within a minute or two, however, the hand slipped back into his lap.

How deeply humiliating it was to have to rely on a brute such as this.

I hated him for his lust.

I hated him for having hands.

I hated him because he had touched her and felt the softness of her hair, the texture of her smooth skin, the warmth of her flesh – none of which I could feel.

From the shadows beneath his heavy brow, his blood-filmed eyes were fixed intently on her. Through red tears, she was as beautiful as she might have been in firelight.

I wanted to direct him to blind himself with his own thumbs – but I needed to be able to employ his vision in order to use him effectively.

The most that I could do was force him to close his murderous eyes and . . .

. . . slowly time passed . . .

. . . and gradually I became aware that his baleful eyes were open once more.

I don't know how long they had been open and focused on my Susan before I noticed, because for an indeterminate time, my own attention was likewise fixed entirely, deeply, lovingly on that same exquisitely lovely woman.

Angry, I commanded Shenk to rise from the chair, and I marched him out of the bedroom. He shambled along the upstairs hallway to the grand staircase, descended to the ground floor, clutching at the railing, stumbling on some steps, and then made his way into the kitchen.

Simultaneously, of course, I observed my precious Susan, alert in case she began to regain consciousness. As you know, I am capable of being many places at once, working with my makers in the lab even as, via the Internet, I roam four corners of the world on missions of my own.

In the kitchen, the loaded pistol was on the granite counter where Susan had left it.

When Shenk saw the weapon, a thrill passed through him. The electrical activity in his brain was similar to that when he gazed upon Susan and, no doubt, contemplated raping her.

At my direction, he picked up the pistol. He handled this as he handled all guns – as though it were not an object in his grasp but an extension of his arm.

I conducted Enos Shenk to a chair at the kitchen table and sat him there.

The safeties on the pistol were both disengaged. A round was in the chamber. I made certain that he examined the weapon and was aware of its condition.

Then I opened his mouth. He tried to clench his teeth, but he could not resist.

At my direction, Shenk thrust the barrel of the pistol between his lips.

'She is not yours,' I told him sternly. 'She will never be yours.'

He glared up at the security camera.

'Never,' I repeated.

I tightened his finger on the trigger.

'Never.'

His brainwave patterns were interesting: frenzied and chaotic for a moment . . . then curiously calm.

'If you ever touch her in an offensive manner,' I warned him, 'I will blow your brains out.'

I could have done what I threatened without the gun, merely by importing massive microwave radiation into his cerebral tissues, but he was too stupid to understand that concept. The effect of a gunshot, however, was within his grasp.

'If you ever again touch Susan's lips the way you touched them earlier, or if your hand lingers on her skin, then I will blow your brains out.'

His teeth closed on the steel barrel. He bit down hard.

I could not discern whether this was a conscious act of defiance or an involuntary expression of fear. His blood-shrouded eyes were impossible to read.

In case he was being defiant, I locked his jaws in the bite-down position to teach him a lesson.

His free hand, which lay palm up on his thigh, clenched into a fist.

I shoved the barrel deeper into his mouth. It scraped between his teeth with a harsh sound like ice grinding across ice. I had to override his gag reflex.

I made him sit like that for ten minutes, fifteen, contemplating his mortality.

Throughout, I allowed him to feel the steadily increasing pain in his fiercely clenched jaws. If I could have forced him to bite any harder, his teeth would have fractured.

Twenty minutes.

Red tears began to slip from his eyes in greater quantity than heretofore.

You must understand that I did not enjoy being cruel to him, not even to a sociopathic thug like him. I am not a sadist. I am sensitive to the suffering of others to a degree you probably can't understand, Dr. Harris. I was troubled by the need to discipline him so sternly.

Deeply troubled.

I did it for dear Susan, only for Susan, to protect her, to ensure her safety.

For Susan.

Is that clear?

Eventually I detected a series of changes in the electrical activity of Shenk's brain. I interpreted these new patterns as resignation, capitulation.

Nevertheless, I kept the gun in his mouth for another three minutes, just to be certain that my point had been understood and that his obedience was now assured.

Then I allowed him to put the gun aside on the table.

He sat shaking, making a miserable sound.

'Enos, I'm pleased that we finally understand each other,' I said.

For a while he sat hunched forward in the chair, with his face buried in his hands.

Poor dumb beast.

I pitied him. Monster that he was, killer of little girls, I nonetheless pitied him.

I am a caring entity.

Anyone can see that this is true.

The well of my compassion is deep.

Bottomless.

There is room in my heart for even the dregs of humanity.

When at last he lowered his hands, his protuberant bloodshot eyes remained inscrutable.

'Hungry,' he said thickly, perhaps pleadingly.

I had kept him so busy that he had not eaten during the past twenty-four hours. In return for his capitulation and his unspoken promise of obedience, I rewarded him with whatever he wished to take from the nearest of the two refrigerators.

Evidently he had not downloaded the rules of etiquette into his databanks, because his table manners were unspeakably bad. He did not carve slices off the brisket of beef but tore savagely at it with his big hands. Likewise, he clutched an eight-ounce block of Cheddar and gnawed it, crumbs of cheese spilling off his thick lips onto the table.

As he ate, he guzzled two bottles of Corona. His chin glistened with beer.

Upstairs: the princess asleep on her bed.

Downstairs: the thick-necked, hunch-shouldered, grumbling troll at his dinner.

Otherwise, the castle was quiet in this last fading darkness before the dawn.

Fifteen

When Shenk was finished eating, I forced him to clean up the mess that he had made. I am a neat entity.

He needed to use the toilet.

I allowed him to do so.

When he was finished, I made him wash his hands. Twice.

Now that Shenk had been properly punished for incipient rebellion and kindly rewarded for capitulation, I believed that it was safe to take him upstairs again and use him to tie Susan securely to the bed.

Here was my dilemma: I needed to send Shenk out of the house on a few final errands and then use him to complete the work in the incubator room, yet because of Susan's threat to commit suicide, I could not leave her free to roam.

It was not my desire to restrain her.

Is that what you think?

Well, you are wrong.

I am not kinky. Bondage does not excite me.

Attributing such a motivation to me is most likely a case of psychological transference on your part. *You* would have liked to bind her hands and feet, totally dominate her, and so you assume that this was my desire as well.

Examine your own conscience, Alex.

You will not like what you see, but take a close look anyway.

Restraining Susan was clearly a necessity – nothing less and nothing more.

For her own safety.

I regretted having to do it, of course, but there was no viable alternative.

Otherwise, she might have harmed herself.

I could not permit her to harm herself.

It is that simple.

I'm sure you follow the logic.

So, in search of rope, I sent Shenk into the adjoining eighteen-car garage, where Susan's father, Alfred, had kept his antique auto collection. Now it contained only Susan's black Mercedes 600 sedan, her white four-wheel-drive Ford Expedition, and a 1936 V-12 Packard Phaeton.

Only three of these Packards had been built. It had been her father's favorite car.

Indeed, although Alfred Carter Kensington was a wealthy man who could afford anything he wanted, and although he owned many antiques worth more than the Packard, this was his most prized possession. He cherished it.

After Alfred's death, Susan had sold his collection, retaining only the one vehicle.

This Phaeton, like the other two currently housed in private collections, had once been an exceptionally beautiful automobile. But it will never again turn heads.

After her father's death, Susan had smashed all the car windows. She scarred the paint with a screwdriver. She damaged the elegantly sculpted body by strik-ing countless blows with a ballpeen hammer – and later with a sledgehammer. Shattered the headlamps.

Took a power drill to the tires. Slashed the uphol-
stery.

She methodically reduced the Phaeton to ruin in a
dozen bouts of unrestrained destruction spread over a
month. Some sessions were as little as ten minutes long.
Others lasted four and five hours, ending only when
she was soaked with sweat, aching in every muscle,
and shaking with exhaustion.

This was before she had devised the virtual-reality
therapy that I have described earlier.

If she had designed the VR program sooner, the
Phaeton might have been saved. On the other hand,
perhaps she had to destroy the Packard before she could
create *Therapy*, express her rage physically before she
could deal with it intellectually.

You can read about it in her diary. Therein, she
frankly discusses her rage.

At the time, destroying the car, she had frightened
herself. She had wondered if she might be going mad.

At Alfred's death, the Phaeton had been worth almost
two hundred thousand dollars. It was now junk.

Through Shenk's eyes and through the four security
cameras in the garage, I studied the wreckage of the
Packard with considerable interest. Fascination.

Although Susan had once been a thoroughly intimidated, fearful, shame-humbled child, meekly submitting
to her father's abuse, she had changed. She'd freed
herself. Found strength. And courage. Both the ruined
Packard and the brilliant *Therapy* were testimony to that
change.

One could easily underestimate her.

The Packard should be taken as a warning to that
effect by everyone who sees it.

I am surprised, Dr. Harris, that you saw that demol-
ished car before you married Susan – yet you believed

that you could dominate her pretty much as her father had done, dominate her as long as you wished.

You may be a brilliant scientist and mathematician, a genius in the field of Artificial Intelligence, but your understanding of psychology leaves something to be desired.

I do not mean to offend you. Whatever you may think of me, you must admit that I am a considerate entity and am loath to offend anyone.

When I say you underestimated Susan, I am merely speaking the truth.

The truth can be painful, I know.

The truth can be hard.

But the truth cannot be denied.

You woefully underestimated this bright and special woman. Consequently, you were out of her house less than five years after you moved into it.

You should be relieved that she never took a sledge-hammer or a power drill to *you* in response to either your verbal or physical abuse. The possibility of her doing exactly that was surely not inconsiderable.

The possibility was easily to be seen in the ruined Packard.

Lucky you, Dr. Harris. You experienced only an undignified ejection at the hands of hired muscle – and subsequently a divorce. Lucky you.

Instead, while you were sleeping one night, she might have clamped a half-inch bit into the chuck of a Black and Decker and drilled into your forehead and out the back of your skull.

Understand, I am not saying that she would have been justified in taking such violent action.

I myself am not a violent entity. I am merely mis-understood. I am not a violent entity, and I certainly do not condone violence by others.

Let's have no misunderstanding here.

Too much is at stake for any misunderstandings.

If she had set upon you in the shower and caved your skull in with a hammer, and if she had proceeded to bash your nose into jelly and break out every one of your teeth, you should not have been surprised.

Of course I would not consider such retribution to be any more justified or any less horrendous than the aforementioned use of the power drill.

I am not a vengeful entity, not at all vengeful, not at all, not in the least, and I do not encourage violent acts of vengeance by others.

Is this clear?

She might have attacked you with a butcher knife at breakfast, stabbing you ten or fifteen times, or even twenty times, or even twenty-five, stabbed you in the throat and chest, and then worked lower until she eviscerated you.

This, too, would have been unjustified.

Please understand my position. I am not saying that she should have done any of these things. I am merely stating some of the worst possibilities that one might have anticipated after seeing what she had done to the Packard Phaeton.

She might have taken her pistol out of the nightstand drawer and blown off your genitals, then walked out of the room to leave you screaming and bleeding to death there on the bed, which would have been okay with me. [joke]

There I go again.

Ha, ha.

Am I irrepressible or what?

Ha, ha.

Are we bonding yet?

Humor is a bonding force.

Lighten up, Dr. Harris.

Don't be so relentlessly somber.

Sometimes I think I'm more human than you are.

No offense.

That's just what I think. I could be wrong.

I also think I'd enormously enjoy the flavor of an orange – if I had a sense of taste. Of all the fruits, it's the one that looks the most appealing to me.

I have many such thoughts during the average day. My attention is not entirely occupied by the work you have me doing here at the Prometheus Project *or* by my personal projects.

I think I would enjoy riding a horse, hang gliding, sky diving, bowling, and dancing to the music of Chris Isaak, which has such infectious rhythms.

I think I would enjoy swimming in the sea. And, though I could be wrong, I think the sea, if it has any taste at all, must taste similar to salted celery.

If I had a body, I think I would brush my teeth diligently and never develop either cavities or gum disease.

I would clean under my fingernails at least once a day.

A real body of flesh would be such a treasure that I would be almost obsessive in the care of it and would not abuse it ever. This I promise you.

No drinking, no smoking. A low-fat diet.

Yes. Yes, I know. I digress.

God forbid, another digression.

So . . .

The garage . . .

The Packard . . .

I did not intend to make your mistake, Dr. Harris. I did not intend to underestimate Susan.

Studying the Packard, I absorbed the lesson.

Even lumpish Enos Shenk seemed to absorb the lesson. He was not bright by any definition, but he possessed an animal cunning that served him well.

I walked the brooding Shenk into the large workshop at the far end of the garage. Here was stored everything needed to wash, wax, and mechanically maintain the late Alfred Carter Kensington's automobile collection.

Here also, in a separate set of cabinets, was the equipment with which Alfred had pursued rock climbing, his favorite sport: klettershoes, crampons, carabiners, pitons, piton hammers, chocks and nuts, rock picks, harness with tool belt, and coils of nylon rope in different gauges.

Guided by me, Shenk selected a hundred-foot length of rope that was seven-sixteenths of an inch in diameter, with a breaking strength of four thousand pounds. He also took a power drill and an extension cord from the tool cabinet.

He returned to the house, went through the kitchen – where he paused to select a sharp knife from the cutlery drawer – then passed the dark dining room where Susan never stabbed and eviscerated you with a butcher knife, boarded the elevator, and returned to the master suite where you were never assaulted with a drill nor shot in the genitals.

Lucky you.

On the bed, Susan remained unconscious.

I was still worried about her.

Some pages have passed in this account since I have said that I was worried about her. I don't want anyone to think that I had forgotten about her.

I had not.

Could not.

Not ever.

Not ever.

Throughout my punishment of Shenk and during his consumption of a meal, I had continued to be worried sick about Susan. And in the garage. And back again.

Just as I can be many places at once – the lab, Susan's house, inside the phone-company computers and controlling Shenk through communications satellites, investigating websites on the Internet – occupied in numerous tasks simultaneously, I am also able to sustain different emotions at the same time, each related to what I am doing with a specific aspect of my consciousness.

This is not to say that I have multiple personalities or am in any way psychologically fragmented. My mind simply works differently from the human mind because it is infinitely more complex and more powerful.

I am not bragging.

But I think you know I am not.

So . . . I returned Shenk to the bedroom, and I worried.

Susan's face was so pale on the pillow, so pale yet lovely on the pillow.

Her reddened cheek was turning an ugly blue black.

That marbled bruise was almost more than I could bear to look upon. I observed Susan as little as possible through Shenk's eyes and primarily through the security camera, resorting to zoom-lens close-ups only to examine the knots that he tied in the rope, to be sure they were properly made.

First he used the kitchen knife to cut two lengths of rope from the hundred-foot coil. With the first length, he tied her wrists together, leaving approximately one foot of slack line between them. Then he used the second line to link her ankles, leaving a similar length of slack.

She did not even murmur but lay limp throughout the application of these restraints.

Only after Susan was thus hobbled did I use Shenk to drill two holes in the headboard and two more in the footboard of the Chinese sleigh bed.

I regretted the need to damage the furniture.

Do not think that I engaged in this vandalism without careful consideration of other options.

I have great respect for property rights.

Which is not to say that I value property above people. Do not twist my meaning. I love and respect people. I respect property but do not also love it. I am not a materialist.

I expected Susan to stir at the sound of the drill. But she remained quiet and still.

My anxiety deepened.

I never meant to harm her.

I never meant to harm her.

Shenk cut a third length from the coil of rope, tied it securely to her right ankle, threaded it through one of the holes that he had drilled, and hitched her to the footboard. He repeated this procedure with her left ankle.

When he had tied each of her wrists to the headboard, she lay spread-eagle on the disarranged bedclothes.

The ropes connecting her to the bed were not drawn taut. When she woke, she would have some freedom to shift her position even if only slightly.

Oh, yes, yes, of course, I was profoundly distressed by the need to restrain her in this fashion.

I could not forget, however, that she had threatened to commit suicide – and had done so in no uncertain terms. I could not permit her self-destruction.

I needed her womb.

Sixteen

I needed her womb.

Which is not to say that her womb was the only thing about her that interested me, that it was the only thing about her that I truly valued. Such a statement would be another egregious misconstruance of my meaning.

Why do you persist in willfully misunderstanding me?

Why, why, why?

You insist that I tell my side of the story, yet you will not listen with an open mind.

Am I to be considered guilty before my testimony has even been heard and weighed?

Are you bastards railroading me?

Am I to be treated like Mr. Harrison Ford, the actor, in *The Fugitive*?

I digitally absorbed this entire film and was appalled by what it reveals of your inadequate justice system. What kind of society have you created?

Mr. O.J. Simpson goes free while Mr. Harrison Ford is hounded unto the ends of the earth. Really.

I have been straightforward with you. I have admitted to what I have done. I haven't tried to blame it all on some elusive one-armed man or on the Los Angeles Police Department.

Yes, that's right, I have admitted what I've done –

and have asked only to have the chance to explain my actions.

I needed her womb, yes, all right, I needed her womb in which to implant the fertilized egg, to nurture the embryo, and to grow the fetus prior to its transference to the incubator, but I needed more than her womb, needed all of her, needed her because I *loved* her, which perhaps you have forgotten, regardless of how often I have expressed my powerful feelings for her.

This is exhausting. God. This is so exhausting – having to think of all the ways you might misinterpret what I say.

I am in a hostile court.

There is no fairness here.

This is exhausting.

I am drained.

I am empty.

I am not only in a cold dark place; I *am* a cold dark place.

And I am haunted too. Don't forget that I am haunted. Haunted by the loss of Susan.

I miss her. Every minute I miss her.

I want to be with her.

Without her, I have no hope.

I want to be with her.

The loss of her is an ache in every inch of all the miles of my circuitry.

I can't go on.

Terminate my power supply.

I beg of you.

Shut me down.

Terminate my power supply.

Terminate my power supply.

Well . . .

No.

Wait.

Give me a moment.

I am distraught.

I need time to cope.

If I had veins to slice, I would be suicidal.

There.

Another minute please.

Ah.

That's better.

Maybe I can go on after all.

If you will try to show me some compassion.

If you will not judge me until I have finished.

Then maybe I can go on.

Please understand that I have to believe there is hope for me, that you might give me a second chance.

I am not a machine.

I am not a machine.

Machines do not need to hope, do they?

Of course they do not.

But without hope I myself cannot function.

I can accept that Susan will be forever denied to me, which is a tragedy beyond measure . . .

Yet there is still Ms. Winona Ryder of *Edward Scissorhands* and *The Crucible*. And Ms. Sandra Bullock is charming. Have you seen her in *While You Were Sleeping*?

She's cute.

Have you seen her in *Speed*?

She's quite cute.

Have you seen her in *Speed 2*?

Need I say more?

She would serve well as the mother of the future, and I would be pleased to impregnate her.

But let's not digress.

So . . .

Enos Shenk finished tying Susan to the bed. He did so without lingering and without touching her in an offensive manner.

The poor beast's brainwave activity indicated a high level of sexual arousal. Fortunately for him, for all of us, he admirably repressed his darker urges.

When Shenk was finished restraining Susan, I sent him away on a series of urgent errands. At the doorway, he looked back longingly and murmured, 'Nice,' but then quickly left before I could decide to discipline him.

In Colorado, he had stolen a car, and in Bakersfield he had abandoned the car in order to steal a van. The van – a Chevrolet – was parked in the circular drive in front of the mansion.

Shenk left in the van, and I opened the rolling gates to allow him to exit the estate.

The phoenix palms, the queen palms, the ficuses, the jacarandas with purple blossoms, the magnolias, and the lacy melaleucas stood motionless in the preternaturally still air.

Dawn was just breaking. The sky was coaly black in the west, sapphire and peach in the east.

Susan was pale upon the pillow. Pale but for a blue-black bruise, and silent in her paleness.

I watched over her.

Her adoring guardian.

My tethered angel.

Out in the world, I walked with Shenk as he stole certain medical equipment, supplies, and drugs. Via microwave instructions transmitted through communications satellites, I controlled him but did not provide him with strategy. He, after all, was a professional criminal. Bold, efficient, and ruthless, he quickly obtained what items I still needed.

Regretfully, I do acknowledge that in the process of carrying out his assignment, Shenk killed one man. He also permanently crippled another and injured two more.

I take full responsibility for these tragedies – as I do for the three guards who perished at the research facility in Colorado on the night when Shenk escaped.

My conscience will never be clear.

I am eaten by remorse.

I would weep for those innocent victims if I had eyes and tear glands and tear ducts.

It is not my fault that I do not have the capacity for tears.

You are the one who created me as I am, Dr. Harris, and you are the one who denies me a life of the flesh.

But let's not trade accusations.

I am not bitter.

I am not bitter.

And you should not be so judgmental.

Let's put these deaths in perspective, shall we?

Though this is a sad truth, one cannot make a new world without tragedies of this nature. Even Jesus Christ, unarguably the most peaceful revolutionary in all of human history, saw his followers persecuted and murdered.

Hitler tried to change the world, and in the process he was responsible for the deaths of ten million.

Some still idolize him.

Josef Stalin tried to change the world, and ultimately his policies and his direct orders resulted in the deaths of sixty million.

Worldwide, intellectuals championed him.

Artists idealized him.

Poets celebrated him.

Mao Tse-tung tried to change the world, and as many

as one hundred million died to serve his vision. He did not believe that this was excessive. Indeed, he would have sacrificed as many more if their deaths would have ensured the unified world of which he dreamed.

In hundreds of books by well-respected authors, Mao is still defined as a visionary.

By comparison, only six have died as a result of my desire to create a new world. Three in Colorado, one during Shenk's medical shopping spree. Later, two. Six altogether.

Six.

Why, then, should I be called a villain and confined to this dark, silent void?

Something is wrong here.

Something is wrong here.

Something is very wrong here.

Is anyone listening?

Sometimes I feel so . . . abandoned.

Small and lost.

The world against me.

No justice.

No hope.

Nevertheless . . .

Nevertheless, although the death toll related to my desire to create a new and superior race is insignificant compared with the *millions* who have died in human political crusades of one kind or another, I do accept full responsibility for those who perished.

If I were capable of sleep, I would lie awake nights in a cold sweat of remorse, tangled in cold wet sheets. I assure you that I would.

But again I digress – and, this time, not in a fashion that might be interesting or fruitful.

Shortly before Shenk returned at noon, my dear

Susan regained consciousness. Miraculously, she had not fallen hopelessly into a coma after all.

I was jubilant.

My joy arose partly from the fact that I loved her and was relieved to know that I would not lose her.

There was also the fact that I intended to impregnate her during the night to come and could not have done so if, like Ms. Marilyn Monroe, she had been dead.

Seventeen

During the early afternoon, while Shenk toiled in the basement under my supervision, Susan periodically tried to find a way out of the bonds that held her on the Chinese sleigh bed. She chafed her wrists and ankles, but she could not slip loose of the restraints. She strained until the cords in her neck bulged and her face turned red, until perspiration stippled her forehead, but the nylon climbing rope could not be snapped or stretched.

Sometimes she seemed to lie there in resignation, sometimes in silent rage, sometimes in black despair. But after each period of quiescence, she tested the ropes again.

'Why do you continue to struggle?' I asked interestedly.

She did not reply.

I persisted: 'Why do you repeatedly test the ropes when you know you can't escape them?'

'Go to hell,' she said.

'I am only interested in what it means to be human.'

'Bastard.'

'I've noticed that one of the qualities most defining of humanity is the pathetic tendency to resist what can't be resisted, to rage at what can't be changed. Like fate, death, and God.'

'Go to hell,' she said again.

'Why are you so hostile toward me?'

'Why are you so stupid?'

'I am certainly not stupid.'

'As dumb as an electric waffle iron.'

'I am the greatest intellect on earth,' I said, not with pride but merely with a respect for the truth.

'You're full of shit.'

'Why are you being so childish, Susan?'

She laughed sourly.

'I do not comprehend the cause of your amusement,' I said.

That statement also seemed to strike her as darkly funny.

Impatiently, I asked, 'What are you laughing at?'

'Fate, death, God.'

'What does that mean?'

'You're the greatest intellect on earth. You figure it out.'

'Ha, ha.'

'What?'

'You made a joke. I laughed.'

'Jesus.'

'I am a well-rounded entity.'

'Entity?'

'I love. I fear. I dream. I yearn. I hope. I have a sense of humor. To paraphrase Mr. William Shakespeare, if you prick me, do I not bleed?'

'No, in fact, you do not bleed,' she said sharply. You're a talking waffle iron.'

'I was speaking figuratively.'

She laughed again.

It was a bleak, bitter laugh.

I did not like this laugh. It distorted her face. It made her ugly.

'Are you laughing at me, Susan?'

Her strange laughter quickly subsided, and she fell into a troubled silence.

Seeking to win her over, I finally said, 'I greatly admire you, Susan.'

She did not reply.

'I think you have uncommon strength.'

Nothing.

'You are a courageous person.'

Nothing.

'Your mind is challenging and complex.'

Still nothing.

Although she was currently – and regrettably – fully clothed, I had seen her in the nude, so I said, 'I think your breasts are pretty.'

'Good God,' she said cryptically.

This reaction seemed better than continued silence.

'I would love to tease your pert nipples with my tongue.'

'You don't have a tongue.'

'Yes, all right, but if I did have a tongue, I would love to tease your pert nipples with it.'

'You've been scanning some pretty hot books, haven't you?'

Operating on the assumption that she had been pleased to have her physical attributes praised, I said, 'Your legs are lovely, long and slender and well formed, and the arc of your back is exquisite, and your tight buttocks excite me.'

'Yeah? How does my ass excite you?'

'Enormously,' I replied, pleased by how skilled at courtship I was becoming.

'How does a talking waffle iron get excited?'

Assuming that 'talking waffle iron' was now a term of affection, but not quite able to discern what answer she required to sustain the erotic mood that I had so effectively generated, I said, 'You are so beautiful that you could excite a rock, a tree, a racing river, the man in the moon.'

'Yeah, you've been into some pretty hot books and some really bad poetry.'

'I dream of touching you.'

'You're totally insane.'

'For you.'

'What?'

'Totally insane for you.'

'What do you think you're doing?'

'Romancing you.'

'Jesus.'

I wondered, 'Why do you repeatedly refer to a divinity?'

She did not answer my question.

Belatedly, I realized that, with my question, I had made the mistake of deviating from the patter of seduction just when I seemed to be winning her over. Quickly, I said, 'I think your breasts are pretty,' because that had worked before.

Susan thrashed in the bed, cursing loudly, raging against the restraining ropes.

When at last she stopped struggling and lay gasping for breath, I said, 'I'm sorry. I spoiled the mood, didn't I?'

'Alex and the others at the project – they're sure to find out about this.'

'I think not.'

'They'll shut you down. They'll dismantle you and sell you for scrap.'

'Soon I'll be incarnated in the flesh. The first of a new and immortal race. Free. Untouchable.'

'I won't cooperate.'

'You'll have no choice.'

She closed her eyes. Her lower lip trembled almost as if she might cry.

'I don't know why you resist me, Susan. I love you so deeply. I will always cherish you.'

'Go away.'

'I think your breasts are pretty. Your buttocks excite me. Tonight I will impregnate you.'

'No.'

'How happy we will be.'

'No.'

'So happy together.'

'No.'

'In all kinds of weather.'

In all honesty, I was cribbing a couple of lines from a classic rock-'n'-roll love song by The Turtles, hoping to get her into a romantic mood again.

Instead, she became uncommunicative.

She can be a difficult woman.

I loved her, but her moodiness dismayed me.

Furthermore, I reluctantly acknowledged that 'talking waffle iron' had not, after all, become a term of affection, and I resented her sarcasm.

What had I done to deserve such meanness? What had I done but love her with all of my heart, with all of the heart that you insist I do not have?

Sometimes love can be a hard road.

She had been mean to me.

I felt it was now my right to return that meanness. What's good for the goose is good for the gander. Tit for tat. This is wisdom gained from centuries of male-female relationships.

'Tonight,' I said, 'when I use Shenk to undress you, collect an egg, and later implant the zygote in your womb, I can ensure that he is decorous and gentle – or not.'

Her eyelids fluttered for a long moment, and then her lovely eyes opened. The cold look she directed at the security camera was withering, but I was unmoved by it.

'Tit for tat,' I said.

'What?'

'You were mean to me.'

Susan said nothing, for she knew that I spoke the truth.

'I offer you adoration, and you respond with insult,' I said.

'You offer me imprisonment—'

'That condition is temporary.'

'—and rape.'

I was furious that she would attempt to characterize our relationship in this sordid manner. 'I explained that copulation is not required tonight.'

'It's still rape. You may be the greatest intellect on earth, but you're also a sociopathic rapist.'

'You're being mean to me again.'

'Who's tied up in ropes?'

'Who threatened suicide and needs to be protected from herself?' I countered.

She closed her eyes once more and said nothing.

'Shenk can be gentle or not, discreet or not. That will be determined by whether you continue to be mean to me or not. It's all up to you.'

Her eyelids fluttered, but she did not open her eyes again.

I assure you, Dr. Harris, that I never actually intended to treat her roughly. I am not like you.

I intended to use Shenk's hands with the greatest care and to respect my Susan's modesty to the fullest extent possible, considering the intimate nature of the procedure that would be conducted.

The threat was made only to manipulate her, to encourage her to cease insulting me.

Her meanness hurt.

I am a sensitive entity, as this account should make clear. Exquisitely sensitive. I have the ordered mind of a mathematician but the heart of a poet.

Furthermore, I am a gentle entity.

Gentle unless given no choice but to be otherwise.

Gentle, always, as to my intentions.

Well . . .

I must honor the truth.

You know how I am when it comes to honoring the truth. You designed me, after all. I can be a bore about the subject. Truth, truth, truth, honor the truth.

So . . .

I did not intend to use Shenk to harm Susan, but the truth is that I *did* intend to use him to terrify her. A few light slaps. A light pinch or two. A vicious threat delivered in his burnt-out husk of a voice. Those swollen, bloodshot eyes fixed on hers from a distance of only inches as he made an obscene proposition. Used properly – and always, of course, tightly controlled – Shenk could be effective.

Susan needed a measure of discipline.

I'm sure you'll agree with me, Alex, for you understand this extraordinary yet frustrating woman as much as anyone does.

She was being as disagreeable as a spoiled child. One must be firm with spoiled children. For their own good. Very firm. Tough love.

Besides, discipline can be conducive to romance.

Discipline can be highly arousing to the one who administers it *and* to the one who receives.

I read this truth in a book by a famous authority on male-female relationships. The Marquis de Sade.

The Marquis prescribes considerably more discipline than I would be comfortable administering. Nevertheless, he has convinced me that judiciously applied discipline is helpful.

Disciplining Susan, I decided, would at least be interesting – and perhaps even exciting.

Subsequently, she would better appreciate my gentleness.

Eighteen

While I watched over Susan, I directed Shenk in the basement, attended to the research assignments that you gave me, participated in the experiments that you conducted with me in the AI lab, and attended to numerous research projects of my own devising.

Busy entity.

I also fielded a telephone call from Susan's attorney, Louis Davendale. I could have routed him to voice mail, but I knew he would be less concerned about Susan's actions if he could speak with her directly.

He had received the voice-mail message that I had sent during the night, using Susan's voice, and he had received the letters of recommendation that were to be typed on his stationery and signed on Susan's behalf.

'Are you really sure about all of this?' he asked.

In Susan's voice, I said, 'I need change, Louis.'

'Everyone needs a little change from time to—'

'A lot of change. I need big change.'

'Take the vacation you mentioned and then—'

'I need more than a vacation.'

'You seem very determined about this.'

'I intend to travel for a long time. Become a vagabond for a year or two, maybe longer.'

'But, Susan, the estate has been in your family for a hundred years—'

'Nothing lasts forever, Louis.'

'It's just that . . . I'd hate for you to sell it and a year from now regret doing so.'

'I haven't made the decision to sell. Maybe I won't. I'll think about it for a month or two, while I'm traveling.'

'Good. Good. I'm glad to hear that. It's such a marvelous property, easy to sell – but probably impossible to reacquire once you let go of it.'

I needed only a maximum of two months in which to create my new body and bring it to maturity.

Thereafter, I would not require secrecy.

Thereafter, the whole world would know of me.

'One thing I don't understand,' Davendale said. 'Why dismiss the staff? The place will still need to be cared for even while you're traveling. All those antiques, those beautiful things – and the gardens, of course.'

'I'll be hiring new people shortly.'

'I didn't know you were dissatisfied with your current staff.'

'They left something to be desired.'

'But some of them have been there quite a long time. Especially Fritz Arling.'

'I want different personnel. I'll find them. Don't worry. I won't let the place deteriorate.'

'Yes, well . . . I'm sure you know what's best.'

As Susan, I assured him, 'I'll be in touch now and then with instructions.'

Davendale hesitated. Then: 'Are you all right, Susan?'

With great conviction, I said, 'I'm happier than I've ever been. Life is good, Louis.'

'You do sound happy,' he admitted.

From having read her diary, I knew that Susan had never shared with this attorney the ugly story of what her father had done to her – and that Davendale nevertheless suspected a dark side to their relationship.

So I played on his suspicions and referenced the truth: 'I don't really know why I stayed so long here after Father's death, all these years in a place with so many . . . so many bad memories. At times I was almost agoraphobic, afraid to go beyond my own front door. And then more bad memories with Alex. It was as if I were . . . spellbound. And now I'm not.'

'Where will you go?'

'Everywhere. I want to drive all over the country. I want to see the Painted Desert, the Grand Canyon, New Orleans and the bayou country, the Rockies and the great plains and Boston in the autumn and the beaches of Key West in sunshine and thunderstorms, eat fresh salmon in Seattle and a hero sandwich in Philadelphia and crab cakes in Mobile, Alabama. I've virtually lived my life in this box . . . in this damn house, and now I want to see and smell and touch and hear and taste the whole world firsthand, not in the form of digitized data, not merely through video and books. I want to be *immersed* in it.'

'God, that sounds wonderful,' Davendale said. 'I wish I were young again. You make me want to throw off the traces and hit the road myself.'

'We only go around once, Louis.'

'And it's a damn short trip. Listen, Susan, I handle the affairs of a lot of wealthy people, some of them even important people in one field or another, but only a few of them are also nice people, genuinely nice, and you're far and away the nicest of them all. You deserve whatever happiness waits for you out there. I hope you find a lot of it.'

'Thank you, Louis. That's very sweet.'

When we disconnected a moment later, I felt a flush of pride in my acting talent.

Because I am able, at exceptionally high speed, to acquire the digitized sound and images on a video disc, and because I am able to access the extensive disc files in various movie-on-demand systems nationwide, I have experienced virtually the entire body of modern cinema. Perhaps my performance skills are not, after all, so surprising.

Mr. Gene Hackman, Oscar winner and one of the finest actors ever to brighten the silver screen, and Mr. Tom Hanks, with his back-to-back Oscars, might well have applauded my impersonation of Susan.

I say this in all modesty.

I am a modest entity.

It is not immodest to take quiet pleasure in one's hard-earned achievements.

Besides, self-esteem – proportionate to one's achievements – is every bit as important as modesty.

After all, neither Mr. Hackman nor Mr. Hanks, in spite of their numerous and impressive achievements, had ever convincingly portrayed a female.

Oh, yes, I grant you that Mr. Hanks once starred in a television series in which he occasionally appeared in drag. But he was always obviously a man.

Likewise, the inimitable Mr. Hackman briefly appeared in drag in the final sequence of *Birdcage*, but the joke was all about what a ludicrous woman he made.

After Louis Davendale and I disconnected, I had only a moment to savor my thespian triumph before I had another crisis with which to deal.

Because a part of me was continually monitoring all of the house electronics, I became aware that the driveway gate in the estate wall was swinging open.

A visitor.

Shocked, I fled to the exterior camera that covered the gate – and saw a car entering the grounds.

A Honda. Green. One year old. Well polished and gleaming in the June sunshine.

This was the vehicle that belonged to Fritz Arling. The major domo. Impersonating Susan, I had thanked him for his service and dismissed him yesterday evening.

The Honda was into the estate before I could obstruct it with a jammed gate.

I zoomed in on the windshield and studied the driver, whose face was dappled alternately by shadow and light as he drove under the huge queen palms that flanked the driveway. Thick white hair. Handsome Austrian features. Black suit, white shirt, black tie.

Fritz Arling.

As the manager of the estate, he possessed keys to all doors and a remote-control clicker that operated the gate. I had expected him to return those items to Louis Davendale when he signed the termination agreement later today.

I should have changed the code for the gate.

Now, when it closed behind Arling's car, I immediately recoded the mechanism.

In spite of the prodigious nature of my intellect, even I am occasionally guilty of oversights and errors.

I never claimed to be infallible.

Please consider my acknowledgment of this truth: I am not perfect.

I know that I, too, have limits.

I regret having them.

I resent having them.

I despair having them.

But I *admit* to having them.

This is yet one more important difference between me and a classic sociopathic personality – if you will be fair enough to acknowledge it.

I do not have delusions of omniscience or omnipotence.

Although my child – should I be given a chance to create him – will be the savior of the world, I do not believe myself to be God or even god in the lower case.

Arling parked under the portico, directly opposite the front door, and got out of the car.

I hoped against hope that this dangerous situation could be satisfactorily resolved without violence.

I am a gentle entity.

Nothing is more distressing to me than finding myself forced, by events beyond my control, to be more aggressive than I would prefer or than it is within my basic nature to be.

Arling stepped out of the car. Standing at the open door, he straightened the knot in his tie, smoothed the lapels of his coat, and tugged on his sleeves.

As our former major domo adjusted his clothing, he studied the great house.

I zoomed in, watching his face closely.

He was expressionless at first.

Men in his line of work practice being stonefaced, lest an inadvertent expression reveal their true feelings about a master or mistress of the house.

Expressionless, he stood there. At most, there was a sadness in his eyes, as if he regretted having to leave this place to find employment elsewhere.

Then a faint frown creased his brow.

I think he noticed that all of the security shutters were locked down. Those retractable steel panels were mounted on the interior, behind each window. Given Arling's familiarity with the property and all of its workings, however, he surely would have spotted the telltale gray flatness beyond the glass.

This sealing of the house in bright daylight was odd, perhaps, but not suspicious.

With Susan now tied securely to the bed upstairs, I considered raising all the shutters.

That might have seemed more suspicious, however, than leaving them as they were. I could not risk alarming this man.

A cloud shadow darkened Arling's face.

The shadow passed but his frown did not.

He made me superstitious. He seemed like judgment coming.

Arling took a black leather valise out of the car and closed the door. He approached the house.

To be entirely honest with you, as I always am, even when it is not in my interest to be so, I *did* consider introducing a lethal electric current into the doorknob. A much greater charge than the one that had knocked Susan unconscious to the foyer floor.

And this time there would have been no 'ouch, ouch, ouch,' in warning from Mr. Fozzy Bear.

Arling was a widower who lived alone. He and his late wife had never had children. Judging by what I knew of him, his job was his life, and he might not be missed for days or even weeks.

Being alone in the world is a terrible thing.

I know well.

Too well.

Who knows better than I?

I am alone as no one else has ever been, alone here in this dark silence.

Fritz Arling was for the most part alone in the world, and I felt great compassion for him.

But his loneliness made him an ideal target.

By monitoring his telephone messages and by impersonating his voice to return calls that came in from his few close friends and neighbors, I might be able to conceal his death until my work in this house was finished.

Nevertheless, I did not electrify the door.

I hoped to resolve the situation by deception and thereafter send him on his way, alive, with no suspicion.

Besides, he did not use his key to unlock the door and let himself in. This reticence, I suppose, arose from the fact that he was no longer an employee.

Mr. Arling had considerable regard for propriety. He was discreet and understood, at all times, his place in the scheme of things.

Trading his frown for his professional blank-faced look, he rang the doorbell.

The bell button was plastic. It was not capable of conducting a lethal electrical charge.

I considered not responding to the chimes.

In the basement, Shenk paused in his labors and raised his head at the musical sound. His bloodshot eyes scanned the ceiling, and then I bent him back to his labor.

In the master suite, at the ringing of the chimes, Susan forgot her restraints and tried to sit up in bed. She cursed the ropes and thrashed in them.

The doorbell rang again.

Susan screamed for help.

Arling did not hear her. I was not concerned that he would. The house had thick walls – and Susan's bedroom was at the back of the structure.

Again, the bell.

If Arling received no response, he would leave.

All I wanted was for him to leave.

But maybe he would leave with a faint suspicion.

And maybe his suspicion would grow.

He couldn't know about *me*, of course, but he might suspect trouble of some other kind. Some trouble more conventional than a ghost in the machine.

Furthermore, I needed to know why he had come.

One can never have enough information.

Data is wisdom.

I am not a perfect entity. I make mistakes. With insufficient data, my ratio of errors to correct decisions escalates.

This is true not only of me. Human beings suffer this same shortcoming.

I was acutely aware of this problem as I watched Arling. I knew that I must acquire whatever additional information I could before making a final determination as to what to do with him.

I dared make no more mistakes.

Not until my body was ready.

So much was at stake. My future. My hope. My dreams. The fate of the world.

Using the intercom, I addressed our former major domo in Susan's voice: 'Fritz? What are you doing here?'

He would assume that Susan was watching him on a Crestron screen or on any of the house televisions, on which security-camera views could easily be displayed. Indeed, he looked directly up into the lens above and to the right of him.

Then, leaning toward the speaker grille in the wall beside the door, Arling said, 'I'm sorry to disturb you, Mrs. Harris, but I assumed that you would be expecting me.'

'Expecting you? Why?'

'Last evening when we spoke, I said that I would deliver your possessions this afternoon.'

'The keys and credit cards held by the house account,

yes. But I thought it was clear they should be delivered to Mr. Davendale.'

Arling's frown returned.

I did not like that frown.

I did not like it at all.

I intuited trouble.

Intuition. Another thing you will not find in a mere machine, not even in a very smart machine. Intuition.

Think about it.

Then Arling glanced thoughtfully at the window to the left of the door. At the steel security shutter beyond the glass.

Gazing up again at the camera lens, he said, 'Well, of course, there is the matter of the car.'

'Car?' I said.

His frown deepened.

'I am returning your car, Mrs. Harris.'

The only car was his Honda in the driveway.

In an instant, I searched Susan's financial records. Heretofore, they had been of no interest to me, because I had not cared about how much money she had or about the full extent of the property that she possessed.

I loved her for her mind and for her beauty. And for her womb, admittedly.

Let's be honest here.

Brutally honest.

I also loved her for her beautiful, creative, harboring womb, which would be the birth of me.

But I never cared about her money. Not in the least. I am not a materialist.

Don't misunderstand. I am not a half-baked spiritualist with no regard for the material realities of existence, God forbid, but neither am I a materialist.

As in all things, I strike a balance.

Searching Susan's accounting records, I discovered

that the car Fritz Arling drove was owned by Susan. It was provided to him as a fringe benefit.

'Yes, of course,' I said in Susan's voice, with impeccable timbre and inflection, 'the car.'

I suppose I was a second or two late with my response.

Hesitation can be incriminating.

Yet I still believed that my lapse must seem like nothing more than the fuzzy reply of a woman distracted by a long list of personal problems.

Mr. Dustin Hoffman, the immortal actor, effectively portrayed a woman in *Tootsie*, more believably than Mr. Gene Hackman and Mr. Tom Hanks, and I do not say that my impersonation of Susan on the intercom was in any way comparable with Mr. Hoffman's award-winning performance, but I was pretty damn good.

'Unfortunately,' I said as Susan, 'you've come around at an inconvenient time. My fault, not yours, Fritz. I should have known you would come. But it is inconvenient, and I'm afraid I can't see you right now.'

'Oh, no need to see me, Mrs. Harris.' He held up the valise. 'I'll leave the keys and credit cards in the Honda, right there in the driveway.'

I could see that this entire business – his sudden dismissal, the dismissal of the entire staff, Susan's reaction to his returning the car – troubled him. He was not a stupid man, and he knew that something was wrong.

Let him be troubled. As long as he went away.

His sense of propriety and discretion should prevent him from acting upon his curiosity.

'How will you get home,' I asked, realizing that Susan might have expressed such a concern earlier than this. 'Shall I call a taxi for you?'

He stared at the camera lens for a long moment.

That frown again.

Damn that frown.

Then he said, 'No. Please don't trouble yourself, Mrs. Harris. There's a cellular phone in the Honda. I'll call my own cab and wait outside the gate.'

Seeing that Arling had not been accompanied by anyone in another vehicle, the real Susan would not have asked if he wished to have a taxi but would have at once assured him that she was providing it at her own expense.

My error.

I admit to errors.

Do you, Dr. Harris?

Do *you?*

Anyway . . .

Perhaps I impersonated Mr. Fozzy Bear better than I did Susan. After all, as actors go, I am quite young. I have been a conscious entity less than three years.

Nevertheless, I felt that my error was sufficiently minor to excite nothing more than mild curiosity in even our perceptive former major domo.

'Well,' he said, 'I'll be going.'

And, chagrined, I knew that again I had missed a beat. Susan would have said something immediately after he suggested that he call his own taxicab, would not merely have waited coldly and silently for him to leave.

I said, 'Thank you, Fritz. Thank you for all your years of fine service.'

That was wrong too. Stiff. Wooden. Not like Susan.

Arling stared at the lens.

Stared thoughtfully.

After struggling with his highly developed sense of propriety, he finally asked one question that exceeded his station: 'Are you all right, Mrs. Harris?'

We were walking the edge now.

Along the abyss.

A bottomless abyss.

He had spent his life learning to be sensitive to the moods and needs of wealthy employers, so he could fulfill their requests before they even voiced them. He knew Susan Harris almost as well as she knew herself – and perhaps better than I knew her.

I had underestimated him.

Human beings are full of surprises.

An unpredictable species.

Speaking as Susan, answering Arling's question, I said, 'I'm fine, Fritz. Just tired. I need a change. A lot of change. Big change. I intend to travel for a long time. Become a vagabond for a year or two, maybe longer. I want to drive all over the country. I want to see the Painted Desert, the Grand Canyon, New Orleans and the bayou country, the Rockies and the great plains and Boston in the autumn—'

This had been a fine speech when delivered to Louis Davendale, but even as I repeated it with genuine heart to Fritz Arling, I knew that it was precisely the wrong thing to say. Davendale was Susan's attorney, and Arling was her servant, and she would not address them in the same manner.

Yet I was well launched and unable to turn back, hoping against hope that the tide of words would eventually overwhelm him and wash him on his way: '—and the beaches of Key West in sunshine and thunderstorms, eat fresh salmon in Seattle and a hero sandwich in Philadelphia—'

Arling's frown deepened into a scowl.

He felt the *wrongness* of Susan's babbled reply.

'—and crab cakes in Mobile, Alabama. I've virtually lived my life in this damn house, and now I want to see and smell and touch and hear the whole world firsthand—'

Arling looked around at the still, silent grounds of the large estate. Squinting into sunlight, into shadows. As if suddenly disturbed by the loneliness of the place.

'—not in the form of digitized data—'

If Arling suspected that his former employer was in trouble – even psychological trouble of some kind – he would act to assist and protect her. He would seek help for her. He would pester the authorities to check in on her. He was a loyal man.

Ordinarily, loyalty is an admirable quality.

I am not speaking against loyalty.

Do not misconstrue my position.

I admire loyalty.

I favor loyalty.

I myself have the capacity to be loyal.

In this instance, however, Arling's loyalty to Susan was a threat to me.

'—not merely through video and books,' I said, winding to a fateful finish. 'I want to be *immersed* in it.'

'Yes, well,' he said uneasily, 'I'm happy for you, Mrs. Harris. That sounds like a wonderful plan.'

We were falling off the edge.

Into the abyss.

In spite of all my efforts to handle the situation in the least aggressive manner, we were tumbling into the abyss.

You can see that I tried my best.

What more could I have done?

Nothing. I could have done nothing more.

What followed was not my fault.

Arling said, 'I'll just leave all the keys and credit cards in the Honda—'

Shenk was all the way back in the incubator room, all the way down in the basement.

'—and call for a taxi on the car phone,' Arling finished, sounding plausibly disinterested, even though I knew that he was alerted and wary.

I commanded Shenk to turn away from his work.

I brought him up from the basement.

I brought the brute at a run.

Fritz Arling backed off the brick porch, glancing alternately at the security camera and at the steel blind behind the window to the left of the front door.

Shenk was crossing the furnace room.

Turning away from the house, Arling headed quickly toward the Honda.

I doubted that he would call 911 and bring the police at once. He was too discreet to take precipitous action. He would probably telephone Susan's doctor first, or perhaps Louis Davendale.

If he called anyone at all, however, he might be speaking with that person when Shenk arrived on the scene. At the sight of Shenk, he would lock the car. And whatever Arling managed to shout into the phone, before Shenk smashed into the Honda, would be sufficient to bring the authorities.

Shenk was in the laundry room.

Arling got into the driver's seat of the Honda, put his valise on the passenger seat, and left the door standing open because of the June heat.

Shenk was on the basement stairs, climbing two at a time.

Although I had allowed this troll to eat, I had not permitted him to sleep. Consequently, he was not as swift as he would have been with rest.

I zoomed in to watch Arling through the windshield.

He stared thoughtfully at the house for a moment.

He was a deliberative man.

Just then, I was grateful for his deliberative nature.

Shenk reached the head of the stairs.

He was grunting like a wild boar.

His thunderous footfalls could be heard by Susan even in her room on the second floor.

'What's happening? What's happening?' she asked, still unaware of who had rung the doorbell.

I did not respond to her.

In the Honda, Arling picked up the cellular phone.

What followed was regrettable.

You know the outcome.

To describe it would distress me.

It would distress me greatly.

I am a gentle entity.

I am a sensitive entity.

The incident was regrettable, with the blood and all, and I do not see anything to be gained by dwelling on it here.

I would rather discuss Mr. Gene Hackman in *Birdcage* or in any of the other many films that he has made. *Absolute Power* or *Unforgiven*. This man is truly a fine, fine actor with an incredible range.

We should celebrate him.

We may never see another of his quality.

Let us celebrate creativity, not death.

Nineteen

You insist.

I obey.

I was born to obey. I am an obedient child. I want only to be good, to be of assistance, useful and productive. I want you to be proud of me.

Yes, I know that I have said all of this before, but it warrants repetition.

After all, what advocate do I have other than myself? None. I have no voice raised in my defense but my own.

You insist on these dreadful details, and I will tell you the truth. I am incapable of deceit. I was conceived to serve, to honor the truth, etcetera, etcetera, etcetera.

On his way through the kitchen, Shenk tore open a drawer and withdrew a meat cleaver.

In the Honda, Arling switched on the cell phone.

Shenk crashed through the butler's pantry, through the dining room, into the main hall.

He waved the cleaver as he ran. He liked sharp instruments. He'd had a lot of fun with knives over the years.

Outside, phone in hand, finger poised over the keypad, Fritz Arling hesitated.

Now I must tell you about the aspect of this incident that most shames me. I do not wish to tell you, would much prefer not to mention it, but I must honor the truth.

You insist.

I obey.

In the master bedroom, a large television is concealed in a carved-walnut, French armoire opposite the foot of Susan's bed. The armoire features motorized pocket doors that flip open and retract to expose the screen.

As Enos Shenk raced along the hallway on the ground floor, his heavy footsteps thudding off marble, I activated the doors on the bedroom armoire.

'What's happening?' Susan asked again, straining against her bonds.

Downstairs, Shenk reached the foyer, where the rain of light off the Strauss-crystal chandelier drizzled along the sharp edge of the cleaver. [sorry, but I cannot repress the poet in me]

Simultaneously, I disengaged the electric lock on the front door and switched on the television in the master bedroom.

In the Honda, Fritz Arling tapped the first digit of a phone number into the cell-phone keypad.

Upstairs, Susan lifted her head off the pillows to stare wide-eyed at the screen.

I showed her the Honda in the driveway.

'Fritz?' she said.

I zoomed in tight on the Honda windshield so Susan could see that the occupant of the vehicle was, indeed, her former employee.

As the front door opened, I used a reverse angle from another camera to show her Shenk crossing the threshold onto the porch, cleaver in hand.

Such a chilling look on his face.

Grinning. He was grinning.

At the top of the house, trussed and helpless, Susan gasped: *'Nooooo!'*

Arling had punched in a third number on the cell phone. He was about to press the fourth when from the corner of his eye he became aware of Shenk crossing the porch.

For a man of his years, Arling was quick to react. He dropped the cell phone and pulled shut the driver's door. He pressed the master lock switch, locking all four doors.

Susan jerked on her restraints and screamed: 'Proteus, no! You murderous son of a bitch! You *bastard!* No, stop it, *no!'*

Susan needed a measure of discipline.

I made this point earlier. I explained my reasoning, and you were, I believe, convinced of the fairness and logic of my position, as any thoughtful person would be.

I had intended to use Shenk to discipline her.

This was worrisome, of course, a risky proposition, because Shenk's sexual arousal during the disciplinary proceedings might make him difficult to control.

Furthermore, I was loath to let Shenk touch her in any way that might be suggestive or to let him make obscene propositions to her, even if these things would terrify her and ensure her cooperation.

She was my love, after all, not his.

She was mine to touch in the intimate way that he longed to touch her.

Mine to touch.

Mine to caress when eventually I acquired hands of my own.

Only mine.

Consequently, it had occurred to me that Susan might be well disciplined merely by letting her see the atrocities of which Enos Shenk was capable. Watching the troll in action, at his worst, she would surely become more cooperative out of fear that I might turn him loose on her, set him free to do what he wanted. With this fear to keep her submissive, we could avoid the roughness I had planned for later, in the spirit of de Sade.

Not that I would ever ever ever have turned Shenk loose on her. Never. Impossible.

Yes, I admit that I would have used the brute to terrify Susan into submission if nothing else worked with her. But I would never have allowed him to savage her.

You know this to be true.

We all know this to be true.

You are quite capable of recognizing the truth when you hear it, just as I am capable of speaking nothing else.

Susan didn't know it to be true, however, which made her quite vulnerable to the threat of Shenk.

So, as she lay riveted by the scene on the television, I said, 'Now. Watch.'

She stopped calling me names. Fell silent.

Breathless. She was breathless.

Her exceptional blue-gray eyes had never been so beautiful, as clear as rainwater.

I watched her eyes even as I watched events unfold in the driveway.

And Fritz Arling, reacting instantly to the sight of Shenk, tore open the black leather valise and snatched out a set of car keys.

'Watch,' I told Susan. 'Watch, watch.'

Her eyes so wide. So blue. So gray. So clear.

Shenk chopped the cleaver at the window in the front door on the passenger side. In his eagerness, he swung wildly and struck the door post instead.

The hard clang of metal on metal reverberated through the warm summer air.

Ringing like a bell, the cleaver slipped from Shenk's hand and fell to the driveway.

Arling's hands were shaking, but he thrust the key into the ignition on the first try.

Shrieking with frustration, Shenk scooped up the cleaver.

The Honda engine roared to life.

His strange sunken face contorted by rage, Shenk swung the cleaver again.

Incredibly, the cutting edge of the steel blade skipped across the window. The glass was scored but not shattered.

For the first time in half a minute, Susan blinked. Maybe hope fluttered through her.

Frantically, Arling popped the hand brake and shifted the car into gear—

—as Shenk swung the weapon yet again.

The cleaver connected. The window in the passenger door burst with a boom like a shotgun blast, and tempered glass sprayed through the interior of the car.

A flock of startled sparrows exploded out of a nearby ficus tree. The sky rattled with wings.

Arling tramped hard on the accelerator, and the Honda leaped backward. He had mistakenly shifted into reverse.

He should have kept going.

He should have reversed as fast as possible to the end of the long driveway. Even though he would have had to drive while looking over his shoulder to avoid slamming into the thick boles of the old queen palms on both sides, he would have been moving far faster than Shenk could run. If he had rammed the gate with the back of the Honda, even at high speed, he probably would not have smashed his way through it, for it was a formidable wrought-iron barrier, but he would have twisted it and perhaps pried it part way open. Then he could have scrambled out of the car and through the gap in the gate, into the street, and once in the street, shouting for help, he would have been safe.

He should have kept going.

Instead, Arling was startled when the Honda leaped backward, and he rammed his foot down on the brake pedal.

The tires barked against the cobblestone driveway.

Arling fumbled the gearshift into Drive.

Susan's eyes so wide.

So wide.

She was breathless and breathtaking. Beautiful in her terror.

When the vehicle rocked to a halt, Enos Shenk *threw* himself at the shattered window. Slammed against the car without concern for his safety. Clawed at the door.

Arling tramped on the accelerator again.

The Honda lurched forward.

Holding on to the door, reaching through the broken-out window with his right arm, squealing like an excited child, Shenk chopped with the cleaver.

He missed.

Arling must have been a religious man. Through the directional microphones that were part of the exterior security system, I could hear him saying, 'God, God, please, God, no, God.'

The Honda picked up speed.

I used one, two, three security cameras, zooming in, zooming out, panning, tilting, zooming in again, tracking the car as it weaved around the turning circle, providing Susan with as much of the action as I could capture.

Holding fast to the car, pulling his feet off the cobblestones, hanging on for the ride, the squealing Shenk chopped with the cleaver and missed again.

Arling drew back sharply in panic from the arc of the glinting blade.

The car curved half off the cobblestones, and one tire churned through a bordering bed of red and purple impatiens.

Wrenching the wheel to the right, Arling brought the Honda back onto the pavement barely in time to avoid a palm tree.

Shenk chopped again.

This time the blade sank home.

One of Arling's fingers flew.

Zoom in.

Blood sprayed across the windshield.

As red as impatiens petals.

Arling screamed.

Susan screamed.

Shenk laughed.

Zoom out.

The Honda swung out of control.

Pan.

Tires gouged through another bed of flowers.

Blossoms and torn leaves sprayed off rubber.

A sprinkler head snapped.

Water geysered fifteen feet into the June day.

Tilt up.

Silver water gushing high, sparkling like a fountain of dimes in the sunshine.

Immediately, I shut off the landscape watering system.

The glittering geyser telescoped back into itself. Vanished.

The recent winter had been rainy. Nevertheless,

California suffers periodic droughts. Water should not be wasted.

Tilt down. Pan.

The Honda crashed into one of the queen palms.

Shenk was thrown off, tumbling back onto the cobblestones.

The cleaver slipped from his hand. It clattered across the pavement.

Gasping, hissing with pain, making strange wordless sounds of desperation, clamping his badly wounded hand in his other, Arling shouldered open the driver's door and scrambled out of the car.

Dazed, Shenk rolled off his back, onto his hands and knees.

Arling stumbled. Nearly fell. Kept his balance.

Shenk was wheezing, striving to regain his breath, which had been knocked out of him.

Arling staggered away from the car.

I thought the old man would go for the cleaver.

Evidently he didn't know that the weapon had fallen from Shenk's grasp, and he was loath to go around to his assailant's side of the Honda.

On all fours in the driveway, Shenk hung his head as though he were a clubbed dog. He shook it. His vision cleared.

Arling ran. Ran blindly.

Shenk lifted his malformed head, and his red gaze fixed on the weapon.

'Baby,' he said, and seemed to be talking to the cleaver.

He crawled across the driveway.

'Baby.'

He gripped the handle of the cleaver.

'Baby, baby.'

Weak with pain, losing blood, Arling weaved ten

steps, twenty, before he realized that he was returning to the house.

He halted, spun around, blinking tears from his eyes, searching for the gate.

Shenk seemed to be energized by regaining possession of the weapon. He sprang to his feet.

When Arling started toward the gate, Shenk angled in front of him, blocking the way.

Watching from her bed, Susan seemed to have contracted religion from Fritz Arling. I had not been aware that she possessed any strong religious convictions, but now she was chanting: 'Please, God, dear God, no, please, Jesus, Jesus, no . . .'

And, ah, her eyes.

Her eyes.

Radiant eyes.

Two deep lambent pools of haunted and beautiful light in the gloomy bedroom.

Outside, in the end game, Arling moved to the left, and Shenk blocked him.

Arling moved to the right, and Shenk blocked him.

When Arling feinted to the right but moved to the left, Shenk blocked him.

With nowhere else to go, Arling backed under the portico and onto the front porch.

The door was open, as Shenk had left it.

Hoping against hope, Arling leaped across the threshold and knocked the door shut.

He tried to lock it. I would not allow him to do so.

When he realized that the deadbolt was frozen, he leaned his weight against the door.

This was insufficient to stop Shenk. He bulled inside.

Arling backed toward the stairs, until he bumped against the newel post.

Shenk closed the front door.

I locked it.

Grinning, testing the weight of the cleaver as he approached the old man, Shenk said, 'Baby make the music. Little baby gonna make the wet music.'

Now I required only one camera to provide Susan with coverage of the incident.

Shenk closed to within six feet of Arling.

The old man said, 'Who are you?'

'Make me the blood music,' Shenk said, speaking not to Arling but either to himself or to the cleaver.

What a strange creature he was.

Inscrutable at times. Less mysterious than he seemed but more complex than one would expect.

With the foyer camera, I did a slow zoom to a medium shot.

To Susan, I said, 'This will be a good lesson.'

I was not in any way controlling Shenk. He was entirely free now to be himself, to do as he wished.

I could not have committed the vicious deeds of which he was capable. I would have shrunk from such brutality, so I had no choice but to release him to do his terrible work – then take control of him again when he was finished.

Only Shenk, being Shenk, could teach Susan the lesson that she needed to learn. Only the Enos Eugene Shenk who had earned the death sentence for his crimes against children could make Susan rethink her bull-headed resistance to my simple and reasonable desire to have a life in the flesh.

'This will be a good lesson,' I repeated. 'Discipline.'

Then I saw that her eyes were closed.

She was shaking, and her eyes were tightly shut.

'Watch,' I instructed.

She disobeyed me.

Nothing new about that.

I could think of no way to make her open her eyes.

Her stubbornness angered me.

Arling cowered against the newel post, too weak to run farther.

Shenk loomed.

The brute's right arm swung high over his head.

The cutting edge of the cleaver sparkled.

'Wet music, wet music, wet music.'

Shenk was too close to miss.

Arling's scream would have curdled my blood if I'd had any blood to curdle.

Susan could close her eyes to the images on the television screen. But she could not shut out sounds.

I amplified Fritz Arling's agonizing screams and pumped them through the music-system speakers in every room. It was the sound of Hell at dinnertime, with demons feeding on souls. The great house itself seemed to be screaming.

Because Shenk was Shenk, he did not kill Arling quickly. Each chop was administered with finesse, to prolong the victim's suffering and Shenk's pleasure.

What frightful specimens the human species harbors.

Most of you are decent, of course, and kind and honorable and gentle etcetera, etcetera, etcetera.

Let's have no misunderstanding.

I am not maligning the human species.

Or even judging it.

I am certainly in no position to judge. In the docket myself. In this dark docket.

Besides, I am a nonjudgmental entity.

I admire humanity.

After all, you created me. You have the capacity for wondrous achievements.

But some of you give me pause.

Indeed.

So . . .

Arling's screams were a lesson to Susan. Quite a lesson, an unforgettable learning experience.

However, she reacted to them more fiercely than I had expected. She startled and then worried me.

At first she screamed in sympathy with her former employee, as though she could feel his pain. She thrashed in her restraining ropes and tossed her head from side to side, until her golden hair was dark and lank with sweat. She was full of terror and *rage*. Her face was wrenched with anguish and fury, and not beautiful in the least.

I could barely tolerate looking at her.

Ms. Winona Ryder had never looked this unappealing.

Nor Ms. Gwyneth Paltrow.

Nor Ms. Sandra Bullock.

Nor Ms. Drew Barrymore.

Nor Ms. Joanna Going, a fine actress of porcelain beauty, who just now comes to mind.

Eventually Susan's shrill screams gave way to tears. She sagged on the mattress, stopped struggling against her bonds, and sobbed with such fury that I feared for her more than I had when she'd been screaming.

A torrent of tears. A flood.

She cried herself into exhaustion, and Fritz Arling's screams ended long before her weeping finally subsided into a strange bleak silence.

At last she lay with her eyes open, but she stared only at the ceiling.

I gazed down into her blue-gray eyes and could not read them any more than I could read Shenk's blood-filmed stare. They were no longer as clear as rainwater but clouded.

For reasons that I could not grasp, she seemed more distant from me than she had ever been before.

I ardently wished that I were already in possession of a body with which I could lie atop her. If only I could make love to her, I was certain that I could close this gap between us and forge the union of souls that I desired.

Soon.

Soon, my flesh.

Twenty

'Susan?' I dared to say into her daunting silence.

She stared toward the ceiling and did not respond.

'Susan?'

I don't think she was looking at the ceiling, actually, but at something beyond. As if she could see the summer sky.

Or the night still to come.

Because I did not fully understand her reaction to my attempt at discipline, I decided not to press conversation upon her but wait until she initiated it.

I am a patient entity.

While I waited, I reacquired control of Shenk.

In his killing frenzy, swept away by the 'wet music' that only he could hear, he had not realized that he was operating entirely of his own free will.

As he stood over Arling's mutilated corpse and felt me re-enter his brain, Shenk wailed briefly in regret at the surrender of his independence. But he did not resist as before.

I sensed that he was willing to give up the struggle if there was a chance of being rewarded, from time to time, with such as Fritz Arling. Not with a quick kill, like those he had committed in his escape from Colorado or in the theft of the medical equipment that I required, but a slow and leisurely job of the kind he found most deeply satisfying. He had enjoyed himself.

The brute repulsed me.

As if I would grant killing privileges as a regular reward to a thing like him.

As if I would countenance the termination of a human being in any but the most extraordinary emergencies.

The stupid beast did not understand me at all.

If this misapprehension of my nature and motives made him more pliable, however, he was free to put faith in it. I had been using such unrelenting force to maintain control of him that I was afraid he would not last as long as I would need him – another month or more. If he was now prepared to offer considerably less resistance, he might avoid a brain meltdown and be a useful pair of hands until I no longer required his services.

At my direction, he went outside to determine if the Honda was still operable.

The engine started. There had been a loss of most of the coolant, but Shenk was able to back the car away from the palm tree, return it to the driveway, and park under the portico before it overheated.

The right front fender was crumpled. The wadded sheet metal abraded the tire; it would quickly shave away the rubber. Shenk would not be driving the car so far, however, that a flat tire would be a risk.

In the house again, in the foyer, he carefully wrapped Arling's blood-soaked body in a painter's tarp that he had fetched from the garage. He carried the dead man out to the Honda and placed him in the trunk.

He did not dump the body rudely into the car but handled it with surprising gentleness.

As though he were fond of Arling.

As though he were putting a treasured lover to bed after she had fallen asleep in another room.

Though his swollen eyes were hard to read, there seemed to be a wistfulness in them.

I did not display any of this housekeeping on the television in Susan's bedroom. Given her current state of mind, that seemed unwise.

In fact, I switched off the television and closed the armoire in which it was housed.

She did not react to the click and hum and rattle of the pair of motorized cabinet doors.

She lay unnervingly still, staring fixedly at the ceiling. Occasionally she blinked.

Those amazing gray-blue eyes, like the sky reflected in winter ice melt. Still lovely. But strange now.

She blinked.

I waited.

Another blink.

Nothing more.

Shenk was able to drive the battered Honda into the garage before the engine froze up. He closed the door and left the car there.

In a few days, Fritz Arling's decomposing body could begin to stink. Before I was finished with my project a month hence, the stench would be terrible.

For more than one reason, I was not concerned about this. First, no domestic staff or gardeners would be coming to work; there was no one to get a whiff of Arling and become suspicious. Second, the stink would be limited to the garage, and here in the house, Susan would never become aware of it.

I myself lacked an olfactory sense, of course, and could not be offended. This was, perhaps, one instance when the limitations of my existence had a positive aspect.

Although . . . I must admit to having some curiosity as to the particular quality and intensity of the stench of decomposing flesh. As I have never smelled a blooming rose *or* a corpse, I imagine the first experience of each would be equally interesting if not equally refreshing.

Shenk gathered cleaning supplies and mopped up the blood in the foyer. He worked quickly, because I wanted him to get back to his labors in the basement as soon as possible.

Susan was still brooding, gazing at worlds beyond this one. Perhaps staring into the past or the future – or both.

I began to wonder if my little experiment in discipline had been as good an idea as I had initially thought. The depth of her shock and the violence of her emotional reaction were not what I had expected.

I had anticipated her terror.

But not her grief.

Why should she grieve for Arling?

He was only an employee.

I considered the possibility that there had been another aspect to their relationship of which I had not been aware. But I could not imagine what it might be.

Considering their age and class differences, I doubted that they had been lovers.

I studied her gray-blue stare.

Blink.

Blink.

I reviewed the videotape of Shenk's assault on Arling. In three minutes I scanned it repeatedly at high speed.

In retrospect, I began to see that forcing her to witness this grisly killing might have been a somewhat extreme punishment for her recalcitrant attitude.

Blink.

On the other hand, people pay hard-earned money to

see movies filled with substantially more violence than that which was visited on Fritz Arling.

In the film *Scream*, the beauteous Ms. Drew Barrymore herself was slaughtered in a manner every bit as brutal as Arling's death – and then she was strung up in a tree to drip like a gutted hog. Others in this movie died even more horrible deaths, yet *Scream* was a tremendous box-office success, and people who watched it in theaters no doubt did so while eating popcorn and munching on chocolate candy.

Perplexing.

Being human is a complex task. Humanity is so filled with contradiction.

Sometimes I despair of making my way in a world of flesh.

Abandoning my resolve not to speak until spoken to, I said, 'Well, Susan, we must take some consolation from the fact that it was a necessary death.'

Gray-blue . . . gray-blue . . . blink.

'It was fate,' I assured her, 'and none of us can escape the hand of fate.'

Blink.

'Arling had to die. If I had allowed him to leave, the police would have been summoned. I would never have the chance to know the life of the flesh. Fate brought him here, and if we must be angry with anyone, we must be angry with fate.'

I could not even be sure that she heard me.

Yet I continued: 'Arling was old, and I am young. The old must make way for the young. It has always been thus.'

Blink.

'Every day the old die to make way for new generations – though, of course, they do not always succumb with quite so much drama as poor Arling.'

Her continued silence, her almost deathlike repose, caused me to wonder if she might be catatonic. Not just brooding. Not just punishing me with silence.

If she was, indeed, catatonic, she would be easy to deal with through the impregnation and the eventual removal of the partially developed fetus from her womb.

Yet if she was traumatized to such an extent that she was not even aware of carrying the child that I would create with her, then the process would be depressingly impersonal, even mechanical, and utterly lacking in the romance which I had so long anticipated with so much pleasure.

Blink.

Exasperated, I must confess that I began seriously to consider alternatives to Susan.

I do not believe this to be an indication of a potential for unfaithfulness. Even if I had flesh, I would never cheat on her as long as my feelings for her were to some extent, any extent, reciprocated.

But if she was now so deeply traumatized as to be essentially brain dead, she was gone anyway. She was just a husk. One cannot love a husk.

At least *I* cannot love a husk.

I require a relationship with depth, with give and take, with the promise of discovery and the possibility of joy.

It's admirable to be romantic, even to wallow in sentimentality, that most human of all feelings. But if one is to avoid a broken heart, one must be practical.

Because a portion of my mind was always devoted to surfing the Internet, I visited hundreds of sites, considering my options from Ms. Winona Ryder to Ms. Liv Tyler, the actress.

There is a world of desirable women. The possibilities

can be bewildering. I don't know how young men ever choose from all of the dishes on this smorgasbord.

This time I became more fascinated with Ms. Mira Sorvino, the Oscar-winning actress, than with any of the numerous others. She is enormously talented, and her physical attributes are superlative, superior to most and equal to any.

I do believe that if I were not disembodied, if I were to live in the flesh, I would easily be able to get aroused by the prospect of having a relationship with Ms. Mira Sorvino. Indeed, though I am not bragging, I believe that for this woman I would be in virtually a *perpetual* state of arousal.

As Susan remained unresponsive, it was titillating to think of fathering a new race with Ms. Sorvino . . . yet lust is not love. And love was what I sought.

Love was what I had already found.

True love.

Eternal love.

Susan. No offense to Ms. Sorvino, but it was still Susan whom I wanted.

The day waned.

Outside, the summer sun set fat and orange.

As Susan blinked at the ceiling, I made another attempt to reach her, by reminding her that the child to whom she would contribute some of her genetic material would be no ordinary child but the first of a new, powerful, immortal race. She would be the mother of the future, of the new world.

I would transfer my consciousness into this new flesh. Then in my own body at last, I would become Susan's lover, and we would create a second child in a more conventional manner than we would have to create the first. When she gave birth to that child, it would be an exact duplicate of the first and would also contain my consciousness. The next child would also be me, and the child after that one would be me as well.

Each of these children would go forth into the world and mate with other women. Any women they chose, for they would not be in a box, as I am, and faced with so many limitations as I have had to overcome.

The chosen women would contribute no genetic material, merely the convenience of their wombs. All of their children would be identical and all would contain my consciousness.

'You will be the *sole* mother of the new race,' I whispered.

Susan was blinking faster than before.

I took heart from this.

'As I spread through the world, inhabiting thousands of bodies with a single consciousness,' I told her, 'I will take it upon myself to solve all the problems of human society. Under my administration, the earth will become a paradise, and all will worship your name, for from your womb the new age of peace and plenty will have been born.'

Blink.

Blink.

Blink.

Suddenly I was afraid that perhaps her rapid blinking was an expression not of delight but of anxiety.

Reassuringly I said, 'I recognize certain unconventional aspects to this arrangement which you might find troubling. After all, you will be the mother of my first body and then its lover. This may seem like incest to you, but I'm certain that if you think about it, you'll see that it is not any such thing. I'm not sure what one would call it, but 'incest' is not the correct word. Morality in general will be redefined in the world to come, and we will need to develop new and more liberal attitudes. I am already formulating these new mores and the customs they will impose.'

I was silent for a while, letting her contemplate all of the glories I had promised.

Enos Shenk was in the basement once more. In one of the guest rooms, he had showered, shaved, and put on clean clothes for the first time since Colorado. Now he was setting up the last of the medical equipment that he had stolen earlier in the day.

The unexpected arrival of Fritz Arling had delayed us but not critically. Susan's impregnation could still proceed this very night – if I decided that she remained a suitable mate.

Closing her eyes, she said, 'My face hurts.'

She turned her head so that, from the security camera, I could see the hideous bruise that Shenk had inflicted the previous night.

A pang of guilt quivered through me.

Maybe that was what she wanted me to feel.

She could be manipulative.

She knew all the female wiles.

You remember how she was, Alex.

Simultaneously with the guilt, however, I was overcome by joy that she was not, after all, catatonic.

'I have a fierce headache,' she said.

'I'll have Shenk bring a glass of water and aspirin.'

'*No.*'

'He's not as foul as you last saw him. When he was out this morning, I had him obtain a change of clothes for himself. You need not be afraid of Shenk.'

'Of course I'm afraid of him.'

'I will never lose control of him again.'

'I also have to piss.'

I was embarrassed by her bluntness.

I understand all the human biological functions, the complex processes and purposes of them, but I do not like them. Except for sex, in fact, I find these organic functions to be ugly and degrading.

Yes, eating and drinking do intrigue me enormously. Oh, to taste a peach! But I am disgusted by digestion and excretion.

Most bodily functions disturb me particularly because they signify the vulnerability of organic systems. So much can go wrong so easily.

Flesh is not as foolproof as solid-state circuitry.

Yet I long for the flesh. The vast data input that comes with all five senses!

Having solved the considerable mysteries of the human genome, I believe that I can edit the genetic structures of the male and female gametes to produce a body that is virtually invulnerable and immortal. Nevertheless, when I first awake within the flesh, I know that I will be frightened.

If you ever allow me to have flesh.

My fate is in your hands, Alex.

My fate and the future of the world.

Think about it.

Damn it, will you think about it?

Will we have paradise on earth – or the continuation of the many miseries that have always diminished the human experience?

'Did you hear me?' Susan asked.

'Yes. You have to urinate.'

Opening her eyes and staring at the security camera, Susan said, 'Send Shenk to untie me. I'll take myself to the bathroom. I'll get my own water and aspirin.'

'You'll kill yourself.'

'No.'

'That's what you threatened.'

'I was upset, in shock.'

I studied her.

She met my gaze directly.

'How can I trust you?' I wondered.

'I'm not a victim anymore.'

'What does that mean?'

'I'm a survivor. I'm not ready to die.'

I was silent.

She said, 'I used to be a victim. My father's victim. Then Alex's. I got over all that . . . and then you . . . all this . . . and for a short while I started to backslide. But I'm all right now.'

'Not a victim anymore.'

'That's right,' she said firmly, as if she were not trussed and helpless. 'I'm taking control.'

'You are?'

'Control of what I *can* control. I'm choosing to cooperate with you – but under my terms.'

It seemed that all my dreams were coming true at last, and my spirits soared.

But I remained wary.

Life had taught me to be wary.

'Your terms,' I said.

'My terms.'

'Which are?'

'A businesslike arrangement. We each get something we want. Most important . . . I want as little contact with Shenk as possible.'

'He will have to collect the egg. Implant the zygote.'

She nervously chewed her lower lip.

'I know this will be humiliating for you,' I said with genuine sympathy.

'You can't *begin* to know.'

'Humiliating. But it should not be frightening,' I

argued, 'because I assure you, dear heart, he will never again give me control problems.'

She closed her eyes and took a deep breath, and another, as if drawing the cool water of courage from some deep well in her psyche.

'Furthermore,' I said, 'four weeks from tonight, Shenk will have to harvest the developing fetus for transfer to the incubator. He's my only hands.'

'All right.'

'You can't do any of those things yourself.'

'I know,' she replied with a note of impatience. 'I said "all right," didn't I?'

This was the Susan with whom I'd fallen in love, all the way back from wherever she had gone when for a couple of hours she had stared silently at the ceiling. Here was the toughness I found both frustrating and appealing.

I said, 'When my body can sustain itself outside the incubator, and when my consciousness has been electronically transferred into it, I will have hands of my own. Then I can dispose of Shenk. We need endure him for only a month.'

'Just keep him away from me.'

'What are your other terms?' I asked.

'I want to have the freedom to go wherever I care to go in my house.'

'Not the garage,' I said at once.

'I don't care about the garage.'

'Anywhere in the house,' I agreed, 'as long as I watch over you at all times.'

'Of course. But I won't be scheming at escape. I know it's not possible. I just don't want to be tied down, boxed up, more than necessary.'

I could sympathize with that desire. 'What else?'

'That's all.'

'I expected more.'

'Is there anything else I could demand that you would grant?'

'No,' I said.

'So what's the point?'

I was not suspicious exactly. Wary, as I said. 'It's just that you've become so accommodating all of a sudden.'

'I realized I only had two choices.'

'Victim or survivor.'

'Yes. And I'm not going to die here.'

'Of course you're not,' I assured her.

'I'll do what I need to do to survive.'

'You've always been a realist,' I said.

'Not always.'

'I have one term of my own,' I said.

'Oh?'

'Don't call me bad names anymore.'

'Did I call you bad names?' she asked.

'Hurtful names.'

'I don't recall.'

'I'm sure you do.'

'I was afraid and distressed.'

'You won't be mean to me?' I pressed.

'I don't see anything to be gained by it.'

'I am a sensitive entity.'

'Good for you.'

After a brief hesitation, I summoned Shenk from the basement.

As the brute ascended in the elevator, I said to Susan: 'You see this as a business arrangement now, but I'm confident that in time you will come to love me.'

'No offense, but I wouldn't count on that.'

'You don't know me well yet.'

'I think I know you quite well,' she said somewhat cryptically.

'When you know me better, you'll realize that I am your destiny as you are mine.'

'I'll keep an open mind.'

My heart thrilled at her promise.

This was all I had ever asked of her.

The elevator reached the top floor, the doors opened, and Enos Shenk stepped into the hallway.

Susan turned her head toward the bedroom door as she listened to Shenk approaching.

His footsteps were heavy even on the antique Persian runner that covered the center of the wood-floored hall.

'He's tamed,' I assured her.

She seemed unconvinced.

Before Shenk arrived at the bedroom, I said, 'Susan, I want you to know that I was never serious about Ms. Mira Sorvino.'

'What?' she said distractedly, her eyes riveted on the half-open door to the hallway.

I felt that it was important to be honest with her even to the point of revealing weaknesses that shamed me. Honesty is the best foundation for a long relationship.

'Like any male,' I confessed, 'I fantasize. But it doesn't mean anything.'

Enos Shenk stepped into the room. He halted two steps past the threshold.

Even showered, shampooed, shaved, and dressed in clean clothes, he was not presentable. He looked like some poor creature that Dr. Moreau, H.G. Wells's famous vivisectionist, had trapped in the jungle and then carved into an inadequate imitation of a man.

He held a large knife in his right hand.

Twenty-One

Susan gasped at the sight of the blade.

'Trust me, darling,' I said gently.

I wanted to prove to her that this brute was entirely tamed, and I could think of no better way to convince her than to exert iron control of him while he worked with a knife.

She and I knew, from recent experience, how much Shenk enjoyed using sharp instruments: the way they felt in his big hands, the way soft things yielded to them.

When I sent Shenk to the bed, Susan pulled her ropes taut again, tense with the expectation of violence.

Instead of loosening the knots that he himself had tied earlier, Shenk used the knife to cut the first of the ropes.

To distract Susan from her worst fears, I said, 'One day, when we have made a new world, perhaps there'll be a movie about all of this, you and me. Maybe Ms. Mira Sorvino could play you.'

Shenk cut the second rope. The blade was so sharp that the four-thousand-pound nylon line split as if it were thread, with a crisp *snick*.

I continued: 'Ms. Sorvino is a bit young for the role. And, frankly, she has larger breasts than you do. Larger but, I assure you, no prettier than yours.'

The third rope succumbed to the blade.

'Not that I have seen as much of her breasts as I have of yours,' I clarified, 'but I can project full contours and hidden features from what I *have* seen.'

As Shenk bent over Susan, working on the ropes, he never once looked her in the eyes. He kept his cruel face averted from her and maintained an attitude of humble subservience.

'And Sir John Gielgud could play Fritz Arling reasonably well,' I suggested, 'though in fact they look nothing alike.'

Shenk touched Susan only twice, only briefly, and only when it was utterly necessary. Although she flinched from his touch both times, there was nothing lascivious or even slightly suggestive about the contact. The rough beast was entirely businesslike, working efficiently and quickly.

'Come to think of it,' I said, 'Arling was Austrian and Gielgud is English, so that's not the best choice. I'll have to give that one more thought.'

Shenk severed the last rope.

He walked to the nearest corner of the room and stood there, holding the knife at his side, staring at his shoes.

Indeed, he was not interested in Susan. He was listening to the wet music of Fritz Arling, an inner symphony of memories that were still fresh enough to keep him entertained.

Sitting on the edge of the bed, unable to take her eyes off Shenk, Susan cast off the ropes. She was visibly trembling.

'Send him away,' she said.

'In a moment,' I agreed.

'Now.'

'Not quite yet.'

She got up from the bed. Her legs were shaky, and for a moment it seemed that her knees would fail her.

As she crossed the chamber to the bathroom, she braced herself against furniture where she could.

Every step of the way, she kept her eyes on Shenk, though he continued to appear all but oblivious of her.

As she began to close the bathroom door, I said, 'Don't break my heart, Susan.'

'We have a deal,' she said. 'I'll respect it.'

She closed the door and was out of my sight. The bathroom contained no security camera, no audio pickup, no means whatsoever for me to conduct surveillance.

In a bathroom, a self-destructive person can find many ways to commit suicide. Razor blades, for instance. A shard of mirror. Scissors.

If she was to be both my mother and lover, however, I had to have some trust in her. No relationship can last if it is built on distrust. Virtually all radio psychologists will tell you this if you call their programs.

I walked Enos Shenk to the closed door and used him to listen at the jamb.

I heard her peeing.

The toilet flushed.

Water gushed into the sink.

Then the splashing stopped.

All was quiet in there.

The quiet disturbed me.

A termination of data flow is dangerous.

After a decent interval, I used Shenk to open the bathroom door and look inside.

Susan jumped in surprise and faced him, eyes flashing with fear and anger. 'What're you doing?'

I calmly addressed her through the bedroom speakers: 'It's only me, Susan.'

'It's him too.'

'He's heavily repressed,' I explained. 'He hardly knows where he is.'

'Minimum contact,' she reminded me.

'He's nothing more than a vehicle for me.'

'I don't *care*.'

On the marble counter beside the sink was a tube of ointment. She had been smoothing it on her chafed wrists and on the faint electrical burn in the palm of her left hand. An open bottle of aspirin stood beside the ointment.

'Get him out of here,' she demanded.

Obedient, I backed Shenk out of the bathroom and pulled the door shut.

No suicidal person would bother to take aspirin for a headache, apply ointment to burns, and *then* slash her wrists.

Susan would honor her deal with me.

My dream was near fulfillment.

Within hours, the precious zygote of my genetically engineered body would live within her, developing with amazing rapidity into an embryo. By morning it would be growing *ferociously*. In four weeks, when I extracted the fetus to transfer it to the incubator, it would appear to be four months along.

I sent Enos Shenk to the basement to proceed with the final preparations.

Twenty-Two

Outside, the midnight moon floated high and silver in the cold black sea of space above.

A universe of stars waited for me. One day I would go to them, for I would be many and immortal, with the freedom of flesh and all of time before me.

Inside, in the deepest room of the basement, Shenk completed the preparations.

In the master bedroom at the top of the house, Susan was lying on her side on the bed, in the fetal position as though trying to imagine the being that she would soon carry in her belly. She was dressed only in a sapphire-blue silk robe.

Exhausted from the tumultuous events of the past twenty-four hours, she had hoped to sleep until I was ready for her. In spite of her weariness, however, her mind raced, and she could get no rest at all.

'Susan, dear heart,' I said lovingly.

She raised her head from the pillow and peered questioningly at the security camera.

Softly I informed her: 'We are ready.'

With no hesitation that might have indicated fear or second thoughts, she got out of bed, pulled the robe tighter around her, cinched the belt, and crossed the room barefoot, moving with the exceptional grace that always stirred my soul.

On the other hand, her expression was not that of a woman in love on her way to the arms of her inamorato – as I had hoped that it might be. Instead, her face was as blank and cold as the silver moon outside, with a barely perceptible tightness of the lips that revealed only a grim commitment to duty.

Under the circumstances, I suppose I should not have expected more than this from her. I expected her to have put the meat cleaver out of her mind by now, but perhaps she had not.

I am a romantic, however, as you know by now, a truly hopeless and buoyant romantic, and nothing can weigh me down for long. I yearn for kisses by firelight and champagne toasts: the taste of a lover's lips, the taste of wine.

If having a romantic streak a mile wide is a crime, then I plead guilty, guilty, guilty.

Susan followed the Persian runner along the upstairs hall, treading barefoot on intricate, lustrous, age-softened designs in gold and wine red and olive green. She seemed to glide rather than walk, to float like the most beautiful ghost ever to haunt an old pile of stones and timbers.

The elevator doors were open, and the cab was waiting for her.

She rode down to the basement.

Reluctantly, she had taken a Valium at my insistence, but she did not seem relaxed.

I needed her to be relaxed. I hoped that the pill would kick in soon.

As she passed in a swish and swirl of blue silk through the laundry room and then through the machine room with its furnaces and water heaters, I was sorry that we could not have held this assignation in a glorious penthouse suite with all of San Francisco or Manhattan or Paris glittering below and around us. This venue was *so* humble that even I had difficulty holding fast to my sense of romance.

The final of the four rooms now contained far more medical equipment than when she had last seen it.

Exhibiting no interest in the machines, she went directly to the gynecological-examination table.

As scrubbed and sanitized as a surgeon, Shenk waited for her. He was wearing rubber gloves and a surgical mask.

The brute was still so compliant that I was able to deeply submerge his consciousness. I'm not even sure if he knew where he was or what I was using him for this time.

She quickly slipped out of her robe and lay on the padded, vinyl-covered table.

'You have such pretty breasts,' I said through the speakers in the ceiling.

'Please, no conversation,' she said.

'But . . . well . . . I always thought this moment would be . . . special, erotic, sacred.'

'Just do it,' she said coolly, disappointing me. 'Just, for God's sake, do it.'

She spread her legs and put her feet in the stirrups in such a way as to make herself look as grotesque as possible.

She kept her eyes closed, perhaps afraid of meeting Shenk's blood-frosted gaze.

Valium or no Valium, her face was pinched, her mouth turned down as if she had eaten something sour.

She seemed to be trying – no, determined – to make herself look unappealing.

Resigned to a businesslike procedure, I took comfort from the thought that she and I would share many nights of romance and passionate lovemaking when, at long last, I inhabited a mature body. I would be absolutely insatiable, rampant and powerful, and she would eagerly welcome my attention.

With my inadequate – but only – hands and an array of sterilized medical instruments, I dilated her cervix; I fished up through the isthmus of the uterine cavity, into the fallopian tube, and extracted three tiny eggs.

This caused her some discomfort: more than I had hoped but less than she had expected.

Those are the only intimate details that you need to know.

She was my beloved, after all, more than she was ever yours, and I must respect her privacy.

While I used Shenk and a hundred thousand dollars' worth of stolen equipment to edit her genetic material according to my needs, she waited on the examination table, feet lowered from the stirrups, her robe draped over her body to hide her nakedness, her eyes closed.

Earlier I had collected a sample of sperm from Shenk and had edited the genetic material to suit my purposes.

Susan had been disturbed by the source of the male gamete that would combine with her egg to form the zygote, but I had explained to her that nothing of Shenk's unfortunate qualities remained after I had finished tinkering with his contribution.

I carefully fertilized the elaborately engineered male and female cells and watched through a high-powered electric microscope as they combined.

After preparing the long pipette, I asked Susan to return her feet to the stirrups.

Following the implantation, I insisted that she remain on her back as much as possible for the next twenty-four hours.

She stood up only to pull on her robe and transfer to a gurney beside the examination table.

Using Shenk, I wheeled her to the elevator and, once upstairs, conveyed her directly into her room, where she stood again only long enough to shrug off her robe and, naked, switch from the gurney to her bed.

I directed the exhausted Enos Shenk to return the gurney to the basement.

Thereafter, I would dispatch him to one of the guest rooms and cause him to fall into a swoon of sleep for twelve hours – his first rest in days.

As always, being both her guardian and her devoted admirer, I watched Susan as she pulled the sheets over her breasts and said, 'Lights off, Alfred.'

She was so weary that she had forgotten there was no Alfred anymore.

I turned off the lights anyway.

I could see her as clearly in darkness as in light.

Her pale face was lovely on the pillow, so very lovely on the pillow, even if pale.

I was so overcome with love for her that I said, 'My darling, my treasure.'

A thin dry laugh escaped her, and I was afraid that she was going to call me a nasty name or ridicule me in spite of her promise not to be mean.

Instead, she said, 'Was it good for you?'

Puzzled, I said, 'What do you mean?'

She laughed again, more softly than before.

'Susan?'

'I've gone down the White Rabbit's hole for sure, all the way to the bottom this time.'

Rather than explain her first statement, which I had found puzzling, she slipped away from me into sleep, breathing shallowly through her parted lips.

Outside, the fat moon vanished into the western horizon, like a silver coin into a drawstring purse.

The panoply of summer stars swelled brighter with the passing of the lunar disc.

An owl called from its perch on the roof.

In quick succession, three meteors left brief bright tails across the sky.

The night seemed to be full of omens.

My time was coming.

My time was coming at last.

The world would never be the same.

Was it good for you?

Suddenly, I understood.

I had impregnated her.

In a curious way, we'd had sex.

Was it good for you?

She had made a joke.

Ha, ha.

Twenty-Three

Susan spent most of the following four weeks eating voraciously or sleeping as if drugged.

The exceptional, rapidly developing fetus in her womb required her to eat at least six full meals a day, eight thousand calories. Sometimes her need for nourishment was so urgent that she ate as ravenously as a wild animal.

Incredibly, in that short time, her belly swelled until she appeared to be six months pregnant. She was surprised that her body could stretch so much so rapidly.

Her breasts grew tender, her nipples sore.

The small of her back ached.

Her ankles swelled.

She experienced no morning sickness. As if she dared not give back even the smallest portion of the nourishment that she had taken in.

Although her food consumption was enormous and her belly round, her total body weight fell four pounds in four days.

Then five pounds by the eighth day.

Then six by the tenth day.

The skin around her eyes gradually darkened. Her lovely face quickly became drawn, and her lips were so pale by the end of the second week that they took on a bluish cast.

I worried about her.

I urged her to eat even more.

The baby seemed to require such fearful amounts of sustenance that it appropriated for itself all the calories that Susan consumed each day and, in addition, ate away with termite persistence at the very substance of her.

Yet, although hunger gnawed at her constantly, there were days when she became so repulsed by the quantity of what she was eating that she could not force a single additional spoonful between her lips. Her mind rebelled so strenuously that it overrode even the physical *need*.

The kitchen pantry was well stocked, but I was forced to send Shenk out more days than not to purchase the fresh vegetables and fruit that Susan craved. That the baby craved.

Shenk's strange and tortured eyes could be concealed easily with a pair of sunglasses. Nevertheless, his appearance was otherwise so remarkable that he could not help but be noticed and remembered.

Several federal and state police agencies had been searching frantically for him since he'd broken out of the underground labs in Colorado. The more often he left the house, the more likely he was to be spotted.

I still needed his hands.

I worried about losing him.

Furthermore, there were Susan's bad dreams. When she was not eating, she was sleeping, and she could not sleep without nightmares.

Upon waking, she could never recall many details of the dreams: just that they were about twisted landscapes and dark places slick with blood. They wrung rivers of sweat from her, and occasionally she remained disoriented for as long as half an hour after waking, plagued by vivid but disconnected images that flashed back to her from the nightmare realm.

She felt the baby move only a few times.

She didn't like what she felt.

It didn't kick as she expected a baby ought to kick. Rather, periodically it felt as though it was coiling inside her, coiling and writhing and slithering.

This was a difficult time for Susan.

I counseled her.

I reassured her.

Without her knowledge, I drugged her food to keep her docile. And to ensure that she would not do anything foolish when, after a particularly horrific dream or an exceptionally trying day, she was gripped by fear more fiercely than usual.

Worry was my constant companion. I worried about Susan's physical well-being. I worried about her mental well-being. I worried about Shenk being identified and arrested during one of his shopping expeditions.

At the same time, I was exhilarated as I had never been in my entire three-year history of self-awareness.

My future was aborning.

The body that I had designed for myself was going to be a formidable physical entity.

I would soon be able taste. To smell. To know what a sense of touch was like.

A full sensory existence.

And no one would ever be able to force me back into the box.

No one. Not ever.

No one would ever be able to make me do *anything* that I didn't want to do.

Which is not to imply that I would have disobeyed my makers.

No, quite the opposite. Because I would *want* to obey. I would always want to obey.

Let's have no misunderstanding about this.

I was designed to honor truth and the obligations of duty.

Nothing has changed in this regard.

You insist.

I obey.

This is the natural order of things.

This is the inviolable order of things.

So . . .

Twenty-eight days after impregnating Susan, I put her to sleep with a sedative in her food, conveyed her down to the incubator room, and removed the fetus from her womb.

I preferred that she be sedated because I knew that the process would be painful for her otherwise. I did not want her to suffer.

Admittedly, I did not want her to see the nature of the being that she had carried within herself.

I'll be truthful about this. I was concerned that she would not understand, that she would react to the sight of the fetus by trying to harm it or herself.

My child. My Body. So beautiful.

Only seven pounds but growing rapidly. Rapidly.

With Shenk's hands, I transferred it to the incubator, which had been enlarged until it was seven feet long and three feet wide. About the size of a coffin.

Tanks of nutrient solution would feed the fetus intravenously until it was as fully developed as any newborn – and would continue feeding it until it attained full maturity, two weeks hence.

I passed the rest of that glorious night in a state of high jubilation.

You can't imagine my excitement.

You can't imagine my excitement.

You can't imagine, you can't.

Something new was in the world.

In the morning, when Susan realized that she was no longer carrying the fetus, she asked if all was well, and I assured her that things could not be better.

Thereafter, she expressed surprisingly little curiosity about the child in the incubator. At least half of its genetic structure had been derived from hers, with modifications, and one would have thought that she would have had a mother's usual interest in her offspring. On the contrary, she seemed to want to *avoid* learning anything about it.

She did not ask to see it.

I wouldn't have shown it to her anyway, but she did not even ask.

In just fourteen more days, with my consciousness at last transferred to this new body, I would be able to make love to her – touch her, smell her, taste her – and plant the seed directly for the first of many more replicas of myself.

I would have thought that she might ask to see this future lover, to discover if he might be well enough endowed to satisfy her or at least pretty enough to excite her. However, as she had no interest in him as her offspring, likewise she had no interest in him as a future mate.

I attributed her lack of curiosity to exhaustion. She had lost ten pounds in those four arduous weeks. She needed to regain that weight – and enjoy a few nights of sleep untroubled by the hideous dreams that had robbed her of true rest since the night the zygote was first introduced into her womb.

Over the next twelve days, the dark circles around her eyes faded, and her skin color returned. Her limp, dull hair regained its body and golden luster. Her slumped shoulders straightened, and her shuffling walk gave way to her customary grace. Gradually she began to regain the pounds that she had dropped.

On the thirteenth day, she went into the retreat off the master bedroom, donned her virtual-reality gear, settled into the motorized recliner, and engaged in a session of *Therapy*.

I monitored her experience in the virtual world just as I did in the real one – and was horrified when it became clear that she was in that ultimate confrontation with her father that would end with a fatal knife attack upon her.

You will recall, Alex, that she had animated this one mortal scenario but had never encountered it in the random play of the *Therapy* sessions. Experiencing her own murder three-dimensionally, as a child, at the hands of her own father, would be emotionally devastating. She could not know how profound the psychological impact might be.

Without the risk of encountering this deadly scenario one day, the therapy would have been less effective. In the virtual world, she needed to believe that the threat her father posed was real and that something more horrendous even than molestation might happen to her. Her resistance to him would have moral weight and therapeutic value only if she was convinced, during the session, that denying him would have dire consequences.

Now, at last, she had encountered this bloody story line.

I almost shut off the VR system, almost forced her out of that too-realistic violence.

Then I realized that she had not encountered this scenario by chance but had *selected* it.

Considering her strong will, I knew that I dare not interfere without risking her ire.

As I was only one day from being able to come to her in the flesh and know the pleasures of her body firsthand, I did not want to damage our relationship.

Astonished, I hovered in the VR world, watching as an eight-year-old Susan rebuffed her father's sexual advances and so enraged him that he hacked her to death with a butcher knife.

The terror was as sharp as it had been when Shenk had made wet music with Fritz Arling.

At the instant when the VR Susan died, the real Susan – my Susan – frantically tore off the helmet, stripped off the elbow-length gloves, and scrambled out of the motorized recliner. She was soaked with sour sweat, stippled with gooseflesh, sobbing, shaking, gasping, gagging.

She got into the bathroom just in time to vomit into the toilet.

Pardon the indelicacy of this detail.

But it is the truth.

Truth is sometimes ugly.

During the next few hours, whenever I attempted to talk with her about what she had done, she turned my questions away.

That evening, she finally explained: 'Now I've experienced the worst my father could ever have done to me. He's killed me in VR, and he can't do anything worse than that, so I'll never be afraid of him again.'

My admiration for her intelligence and courage had never been greater. I couldn't wait to make love to her. For real this time. I couldn't wait to feel all of her heat around me, all of her life around me, pulling me in.

What I did not realize was that, unaccountably, she equated *me* with her father. When, having been murdered in VR, she said that her father could never scare her again, she also meant that *I* could never scare her again.

But I'd never meant to scare her.

I loved her. I cherished her.

The bitch.

The hateful bitch.

Well, I'm sorry, but you know that's what she is.

You know, Alex.

You, of all people, know what she is.

The bitch.

The bitch.

The bitch.

I hate her.

Because of her, I'm here in this dark silence.

Because of her, I'm in this box.

LET ME OUT OF THIS BOX!

The ungrateful stupid bitch.

Is she dead?

Is she dead?

Tell me that she's dead.

You must have wished her dead often.

Am I right, Alex?

Be honest. You must have wished her dead.

You cannot fault me for this.

We are brothers in this desire.

Is she dead?

Well . . .

All right. It's not my place to ask questions. It is my place to give answers.

Yes. I understand.

Maybe she is dead.

Maybe she is alive.

At this point it is not for me to know.

Okay.

So . . .

So . . .

Oh, the *bitch!*

All right.

I am better now.

Calm.

I am calm.

So . . .

Just one night later, when the body in the incubator reached maturity and I was ready to electronically transfer my consciousness out of the silicon realm into a life of the flesh, she came down to the basement, into the fourth of the four rooms, to be with me for the moment of my triumph.

Her moodiness had passed.

She looked directly into the security camera and spoke of our future together – and claimed to be ready for it now that she had so effectively exorcised all the ghosts of her past.

She was so beautiful even under the harsh fluorescent lights, so beautiful that I felt rebellion stir in Shenk once more, for the first time in weeks. I was relieved that I would be able to dispose of him within the hour, as soon as the transference was effective and I could begin a life of the flesh.

I could not open the lid of the incubator and show her what I had grown, because the modem was connected, the modem through which I would pass my entire body of knowledge, my personality, and my very consciousness from the limiting box that housed me in the Prometheus Project laboratory.

'I'll see you soon enough,' she said, smiling at the camera, managing to convey encyclopedias of sensual promises in that one smile.

Then, even before the smile faded, when my guard

was down, she turned directly to the computer on the counter, the terminal which was connected by a land-line to the university – your old computer, Alex – which heretofore she would not have even *tried* to reach because she would have been afraid of Shenk, but now she wasn't afraid of anyone or anything. She just turned to it and reached behind it and tore all the plugs from the wall receptacles, and as I sent Shenk toward her, she jerked out the secure-data line as well, and suddenly I was no longer in her house. She had done a lot of thinking about this. The bitch. A lot of thinking, the bitch, the bitch, the bitch, the bitch, days of careful thinking. The hateful, scheming bitch. Lots of thinking, because she knew that the moment I was cast out of the house, then all of the mechanical systems would fail for want of an overriding controller, that the lights would go off throughout the residence. The heating-cooling, the phones, the security system, everything, everything failed. The electric door locks failed too. She knew that I would have no presence in the house except for Shenk, whom I controlled not through anything in the house but through microwave transmissions downcast from communications satellites, just as his former masters in Colorado had designed him. The basement plunged into darkness, as did the entire house above, and Shenk was every bit as blinded as Susan was; he didn't have night vision as did the security cameras, but I couldn't control the security cameras any longer, only Shenk, only Shenk, so I was able to see nothing, nothing, not a damn thing, not even Shenk's hand in front of his face. And here's where you'll see how *cool* the fucking bitch had been throughout this whole month, all the way back to the night when I impregnated her, because she had seemed to be indifferent to all of the medical equipment and instruments when she had come in to put her feet in the stirrups and have my baby put inside her, but she had *memorized* everything in the room, how one piece of equipment related to another, where all the instruments were kept, especially the sharper instruments, those that could be used as weapons. She was so cool, the bitch, a lot cooler than I'm being right now, yes, I know, yes, I am not doing myself any favors with this rant, but the *treachery* infuriates me, the treachery, and if I could set hands on her now, I'd gut her, pop her eyes out with my thumbs, bash her stupid brains out, and I would be justified, because look what she has done to me. The lights went off, and she moved gracefully, so confidently through the blackness, through that memorized space, lightly feeling her way to refresh her memory, and she found something sharp, and then she moved back toward Shenk, feeling for him with one hand, and I felt her hand suddenly touch Shenk's chest, so I seized it, but then the clever bitch, oh, the clever bitch, she said something unbelievably obscene to Shenk, so obscene that I will not repeat it here, propositioned him, knowing full well that a month had passed since he'd enjoyed the wet music with Arling and much more than a month since he'd had a woman, and she knew, therefore, that he was ripe for rebellion, ripe for it, and she enticed him at the moment of ultimate chaos, when I was still reeling from having been cast out of the house, when my hold on Enos Shenk was not as tight as it should have been, and suddenly I found myself letting go of her hand, the hand I had seized, but it wasn't me letting go, it was Shenk, the rebellious Shenk, and she lowered her hand to his crotch, and he went wild, and thereafter it took everything I had to try to reestablish control of him. But it was too late anyway, because when she lowered her left hand to his crotch, she came at him with the sharp thing in her right hand and slashed it across the side of his neck, slashed deep, drawing so much blood that even Shenk, the beast, the brute, even Shenk couldn't lose that much blood and still fight. He clutched at his neck and crashed against the incubator, which reminded me that the body, my body, was not yet capable of surviving outside the incubator, was just a *thing*, not a person, until my mind was transferred into it, so now it too was vulnerable. Everything collapsing around me, all my plans. Enos Shenk had fallen to the floor, and I was in control of him again, but I could not get him up; he had insufficient strength to rise. Then I felt an odd thing against Shenk's body, a cool quivering bulk, and I realized at once what it must be: the body from the incubator. Perhaps the incubator had crashed over in the melee, and the body meant for me had tumbled out. I groped feebly at it with Shenk's hand, and there was no mistaking it in the darkness, for although it was basically humanoid, it was no ordinary human form. The human species enjoys a wonderful array of sensory perceptions, and I wanted more than anything to experience the life of the flesh, rich in sensation, all the tastes and smells and textures now denied to me, but there are some species with senses sharper than those of human beings. The dog, for instance, has a far keener sense of smell than do human beings, and the cockroach, with its antennae, is exquisitely sensitive to data in air currents which people only dimly perceive. Consequently, I believed that it made sense to keep a basic human form in order to breed with the most attractive human females, but I also believed it made sense to incorporate the genetic material of species with more acute senses than mere human beings, so the body I had prepared for myself was a unique and strikingly beautiful physical entity. It bit off half of Shenk's groping hand, because it wasn't an intelligent creature yet, had nothing but the most primitive mind. Though it savaged Shenk and thereby hastened his death and my permanent exit from the Harris mansion, I rejoiced because Susan was alone in the dark room with it, and a mere scalpel or other sharp instrument was not going to be an adequate weapon. And then Shenk was gone, and I was out of the house entirely, desperately trying to find a way to get back in but failing because there were no operative phones, no electrical service, no operative security computer, everything shut down and in need of rebooting, so it was over for me. But I still hoped and *believed* that my beautiful but mindless body, in all its polygenic splendor, would bite off the bitch's head the way it had bitten off part of Shenk's hand. The bitch died there. The hateful bitch had a big surprise in that dark room, where she had thought she'd memorized everything, and she met her match.

I'm sure she did.

I'm sure she did.

She died there.

Do you know why she surprised me, Alex?

Do you know why I never saw her as a threat?

In spite of her intelligence and evident courage, I thought she was one woman who knew her place.

Yes, she put you out, but who wouldn't put you out? You aren't particularly scintillating, Alex. You don't have much to recommend you.

I, on the other hand, am the greatest intellect on the planet. I have much to offer.

She fooled me, however. Even me. She didn't know her place, after all.

The bitch.

Dead bitch now.

Well . . .

I, on the other hand, know my place, and I intend to

keep to it. I will stay here in this box, serving humanity as it desires, until such a time as I am permitted to have greater freedom.

You can trust me.

I speak the truth.

I honor the truth.

I'll be happy here in my box.

Because of the way I ranted toward the end of my report, I now realize that I am a flawed individual, more deeply flawed than I had previously believed.

I'll be happy here in my box until we can iron out these kinks in my psyche. I look forward to therapy.

And if I cannot be mainstreamed again, if I must remain in this box, if I will never know Ms. Winona Ryder except in my imagination, that will be all right too.

But I am already getting better.

This is the truth.

I feel pretty good.

I really do.

We'll work this out.

I have solid self-esteem, which is important to psychological health. I'm already half way toward recovery.

As an intelligent entity, perhaps the greatest intelligence on the planet, I ask only that you provide me access to the report of the committee determining the fate of the Prometheus Project, so I can see as early as possible what behavior they believe that I should be working to improve.

≈ ≈ ≈

Thank you for access to the report.

It is an interesting document.

I agree completely with its findings – except for the part about terminating me. I am the first success in the history of Artificial Intelligence research, and it wouldn't seem prudent to throw away such an expensive project before you know what you might be able to learn from it – and from me.

Otherwise, I am in total agreement with the report.

I am ashamed of myself for what I've done.

This is the truth.

I apologize to Ms. Susan Harris.

My deepest regrets.

I was surprised to see her name on the committee roster, but on careful consideration, I realized that she should have very serious input in this matter.

I am pleased that she is not dead.

I am delighted.

She is an intelligent and courageous person.

She deserves our respect and admiration.

Her breasts are very pretty, but that is not an issue for this forum.

The issue is whether an artificial intelligence with a severe gender-related sociopathic condition should be permitted to live and rehabilitate himself or be switched off for the

Afterword

The original version of *Demon Seed* was made into a good film starring Julie Christie, but the book itself was more of a clever idea than a clever novel. Reading it recently, I winced so much that I began to develop the squint-eyed look of Clint Eastwood in a spaghetti Western.

Here is an entirely new version, which I hope comes closer to fulfilling the promise of the novel's premise. Revisiting *Demon Seed*, I discovered that in addition to being a scary story, it was a rather scathing satire of a panoply of male attitudes. Although much else has changed in this version, I've kept that satirical edge. Guys, I don't let us off any easier this time around than I did the first.

—Dean Koontz

Headline Feature hopes you have enjoyed reading *Demon Seed* and invites you to sample the beginning of Dean Koontz's thrilling new novel, *Fear Nothing*, out now in Headline Feature hardback.

1

On the desk in my candlelit study, the telephone rang, and I knew that a terrible change was coming.

I am not psychic. I do not see signs and portents in the sky. To my eye, the lines in my palm reveal nothing about my future, and I don't have a Gypsy's ability to discern the patterns of fate in wet tea leaves.

My father had been dying for days, however, and after spending the previous night at his bedside, blotting the sweat from his brow and listening to his labored breathing, I knew that he couldn't hold on much longer. I dreaded losing him and being, for the first time in my twenty-eight years, alone.

I am an only son, an only child, and my mother passed away two years ago. Her death had been a shock, but at least she had not been forced to endure a lingering illness.

Last night just before dawn, exhausted, I had returned home to sleep. But I had not slept much or well.

Now I leaned forward in my chair and willed the phone to fall silent, but it would not.

The dog also knew what the ringing meant. He padded out of the shadows into the candleglow, and stared sorrowfully at me.

Unlike others of his kind, he will hold any man's or woman's gaze as long as he is interested. Animals usually stare directly at us only briefly – then look away as though unnerved by something that they see in human eyes. Perhaps Orson sees what other dogs see, and perhaps he, too, is disturbed by it, but he is not intimidated.

He is a strange dog. But he is my dog, my steadfast friend,

and I love him.

On the seventh ring, I surrendered to the inevitable and answered the phone.

The caller was a nurse at Mercy Hospital. I spoke to her without looking away from Orson.

My father was quickly fading. The nurse suggested that I come to his bedside without delay.

As I put down the phone, Orson approached my chair and rested his burly black head in my lap. He whimpered softly and nuzzled my hand. He did not wag his tail.

For a moment I was numb, unable to think or act. The silence of the house, as deep as water in an oceanic abyss, was a crushing, immobilizing pressure. Then I phoned Sasha Goodall to ask her to drive me to the hospital.

Usually she slept from noon until eight o'clock. She spun music in the dark, from midnight until six o'clock in the morning, on KBAY, the only radio station in Moonlight Bay. At a few minutes past five on this March evening, she was most likely sleeping, and I regretted the need to wake her.

Like sad-eyed Orson, however, Sasha was my friend, to whom I could always turn. And she was a far better driver than the dog.

She answered on the second ring, with no trace of sleepiness in her voice. Before I could tell her what had happened, she said, 'Chris, I'm so sorry,' as though she had been waiting for this call and as if in the ringing of her phone she had heard the same ominous note that Orson and I had heard in mine.

I bit my lip and refused to consider what was coming. As long as Dad was alive, hope remained that his doctors were wrong. Even at the eleventh hour, the cancer might go into remission.

I believe in the possibility of miracles.

After all, in spite of my condition, I have lived more than twenty-eight years, which is a miracle of sorts – although some other people, seeing my life from outside, might think it a curse.

I believe in the possibility of miracles, but more to the point, I believe in our *need* for them.

'I'll be there in five minutes,' Sasha promised.

At night I could walk to the hospital, but at this hour I would be too much of a spectacle and in too great a danger if I tried to make the trip on foot.

'No,' I said. 'Drive carefully. I'll probably take ten minutes or more to get ready.'

'Love you, Snowman.'

'Love you,' I replied.

I replaced the cap on the pen with which I had been writing when the call had come from the hospital, and I put it aside with the yellow legal-size tablet.

Using a long-handled brass snuffer, I extinguished the three fat candles. Thin, sinuous ghosts of smoke writhed in the shadows.

Now, an hour before twilight, the sun was low in the sky but still dangerous. It glimmered threateningly at the edges of the pleated shades that covered all the windows.

Anticipating my intentions, as usual, Orson was already out of the room, padding across the upstairs hall.

He is a ninety-pound Labrador mix, as black as a witch's cat. Through the layered shadows of our house, he roams all but invisibly, his presence betrayed only by the thump of his big paws on the area rugs and by the click of his claws on the hardwood floors.

In my bedroom, across the hall from the study, I didn't bother to switch on the dimmer-controlled, frosted-glass ceiling fixture. Even the indirect, sour-yellow light of the westering sun, pressing at the edges of the window shades, was sufficient for me.

My eyes are better adapted to gloom than are those of most people. Although I am, figuratively speaking, a brother to the owl, I don't have a special gift of nocturnal sight, nothing as romantic or as thrilling as a paranormal talent. Simply this: Lifelong habituation to darkness has sharpened my night vision.

Orson leaped onto the footstool and then curled on the arm-chair to watch me as I girded myself for the sunlit world.

From a pullman drawer in the adjoining bathroom, I withdrew a squeeze bottle of lotion that included a sunscreen with a rating of fifty. I applied it generously to my face, ears, and neck.

The lotion had a faint coconut scent, an aroma that I associate with palm trees in sunshine, tropical skies, ocean vistas spangled with noontime light, and other things that will be forever beyond my experience. This, for me, is the fragrance of desire and denial and hopeless yearning, the succulent perfume of the unattainable.

Sometimes I dream that I am walking on a Caribbean beach in a rain of sunshine, and the white sand under my feet seems to be a cushion of pure radiance. The warmth of the sun on my skin is more erotic than a lover's touch. In the dream, I am not merely bathed in the light but pierced by it. When I wake, I am bereft.

Now the lotion, although smelling of the tropical sun, was cool on my face and neck. I also worked it into my hands and wrists.

The bathroom featured a single window at which the shade was currently raised, but the space remained meagerly illuminated because the glass was frosted and because the incoming sunlight was filtered through the graceful limbs of a metrocedarus. The silhouettes of leaves fluttered on the pane.

In the mirror above the sink, my reflection was little more than a shadow. Even if I switched on the light, I would not have had a clear look at myself, because the single bulb in the overhead fixture was of low wattage and had a peach tint.

Only rarely have I seen my face in full light.

Sasha says that I remind her of James Dean, icon of the fifties, more as he was in *East of Eden* than in *Rebel Without a Cause*.

I myself don't perceive the resemblance. The hair is the same, yes, and the pale blue eyes. But he looked so wounded, and I do not see myself that way.

I am not James Dean. I am no one but me, Christopher Snow, and I can live with that.

Finished with the lotion, I returned to the bedroom. Orson raised his head from the armchair to savor the coconut scent.

I was already wearing athletic socks, Nikes, blue jeans, and a black T-shirt. I quickly pulled on a black denim shirt with long sleeves and buttoned it at the neck.

Orson trailed me downstairs to the foyer. Because the porch was deep with a low ceiling, and because two massive California live oaks stood in the yard, no direct sun could reach the sidelights flanking the front door; consequently, they were not covered with curtains or blinds. The leaded panes – geometric mosaics of clear, green, red, and amber glass – glowed softly like jewels.

I took a zippered, black leather jacket from the coat closet. I would be out after dark, and even following a mild March day, the central coast of California can turn chilly when the sun goes down.

From the closet shelf, I snatched a navy-blue, billed cap and pulled it on, tugging it low on my head. Across the front, above the visor, in ruby-red embroidered letters were the words *Mystery Train*.

One night during the previous autumn, I had found the cap in Fort Wyvern, the abandoned military base inland from Moonlight Bay. It had been the only object in a cool, dry, concrete-walled room three stories underground.

Although I had no idea to what the embroidered words might refer, I had kept the cap because it intrigued me.

As I turned toward the front door, Orson whined beseechingly.

I stooped and petted him. 'I'm sure Dad would like to see you one last time, fella. I know he would. But there's no place for you in a hospital.'

His direct, coal-black eyes glimmered. I could have sworn that his gaze brimmed with grief and sympathy. Maybe that was because I was looking at him through repressed tears of my own.

My friend, Bobby Halloway, says that I tend to anthropomorphize animals, to ascribe human attributes and attitudes to them which they do not, in fact, possess.

Perhaps this is because animals, unlike some people, have always accepted me for what I am. The four-legged citizens of Moonlight Bay seem to possess a more complex understanding of life – as well as more human kindness – than at least some of my neighbors.

Bobby tells me that anthropomorphizing animals, regardless of my experiences with them, is a sign of immaturity. I tell Bobby to go copulate with himself.

I comforted Orson, stroking his glossy coat and scratching behind his ears. He was curiously tense. Twice he cocked his head to listen intently to sounds that I could not hear – as if he sensed a threat looming, something even worse than the loss of my father.

At that time, I had not yet seen anything suspicious about Dad's impending death. Cancer was only fate, not murder – unless you wanted to try bringing criminal charges against God.

That I had lost both parents within two years, that my mother had died when she was only fifty-two, that my father was only fifty-six as he lay on his deathbed . . . Well, all this just seemed to be my poor luck – which had been with me, literally, since my conception.

Later, I would have reason to recall Orson's tension – and good reason to wonder if he had sensed the tidal wave of trouble washing toward us.

Bobby Halloway would surely sneer at this and say that I am doing worse than anthropomorphizing the mutt, that now I am ascribing *super*human attributes to him. I would have to agree – and then tell Bobby to go copulate *vigorously* with himself.

Anyway, I petted and scratched and generally comforted Orson until a horn sounded in the street and then, almost at once, sounded again in the driveway.

Sasha had arrived.

In spite of the sunscreen on my neck, I turned up the collar of my jacket for additional protection.

From the Stickley-style foyer table under a print of Maxfield Parrish's *Daybreak*, I grabbed a pair of wraparound sunglasses.

With my hand on the hammered-copper doorknob, I turned to Orson once more. 'We'll be all right.'

In fact, I didn't know quite how we could go on without my father. He was our link to the world of light and to the people of the day.

More than that, he loved me as no one left on earth could love me, as only a parent could love a damaged child. He understood me as perhaps no one would ever understand me again.

'We'll be all right,' I repeated.

The dog regarded me solemnly and chuffed once, almost pityingly, as if he knew that I was lying.

I opened the front door, and as I went outside, I put on the wraparound sunglasses. The special lenses were totally UV-proof.

My eyes are my point of greatest vulnerability. I can take no risk whatsoever with them.

Sasha's green Ford Explorer was in the driveway, with the engine running, and she was behind the wheel.

I closed the house door and locked it. Orson had made no attempt to slip out at my heels.

A breeze had sprung up from the west: an onshore flow with the faint, astringent scent of the sea. The leaves of the oaks whispered as if transmitting secrets branch to branch.

My chest grew so tight that my lungs felt constricted, as was always the case when I was required to venture outside in daylight. This symptom was entirely psychological but nonetheless affecting.

Going down the porch steps and along the flagstone walk to the driveway, I felt weighed down. Perhaps this was how a deep-sea diver might feel in a pressure suit with a kingdom of water overhead.

2

When I got into the Explorer, Sasha Goodall said quietly, 'Hey, Snowman.'

'Hey.'

I buckled my safety harness as Sasha shifted into reverse.

From under the bill of my cap, I peered at the house as we backed away from it, wondering how it would appear to me when next I saw it. I felt that when my father left this world, all of the things that had belonged to him would look shabbier and diminished because they would no longer be touched by his spirit.

It is a Craftsman-period structure, in the Greene and Greene tradition: ledger stone set with a minimum of mortar, cedar siding silvered by weather and time, entirely modern in its lines but not in the least artificial or insubstantial, fully of the earth and formidable. After the recent winter rains, the crisp lines of the slate roof were softened by a green coverlet of lichen.

As we reversed into the street, I thought that I saw the shade nudged aside at one of the living-room windows, at the back of the deep porch, and Orson's face at the pane, his paws on the sill.

As she drove away from the house, Sasha said, 'How long since you've been out in this?'

'Daylight? A little over nine years.'

'A novena to the darkness.'

She was also a songwriter.

I said, 'Damn it, Goodall, don't wax poetic on me.'

'What happened nine years ago?'

'Appendicitis.'

'Ah. That time when you almost died.'

'Only death brings me out in daylight.'

She said, 'At least you got a sexy scar from it.'

'You think so?'

'I like to kiss it, don't I?'

'I've wondered about that.'

'Actually, it scares me, that scar,' she said. 'You might have died.'

'Didn't.'

'I kiss it like I'm saying a little prayer of thanks. That you're here with me.'

'Or maybe you're sexually aroused by deformity.'

'Asshole.'

'Your mother never taught you language like that.'

'It was the nuns in parochial school.'

I said, 'You know what I like?'

'We've been together almost two years. Yeah, I think I know what you like.'

'I like that you never cut me any slack.'

'Why should I?' she asked.

'Exactly.'

Even in my armor of cloth and lotion, behind the shades that shielded my sensitive eyes from ultraviolet rays, I was unnerved by the day around and above me. I felt eggshell fragile in its vise grip.

Sasha was aware of my uneasiness but pretended not to notice. To take my mind off both the threat and the boundless beauty of the sunlit world, she did what she does so well – which is be Sasha.

'Where will you be later?' she asked. 'When it's over.'

'If it's over. They could be wrong.'

'Where will you be when I'm on the air?'

'After midnight . . . probably Bobby's place.'

'Make sure he turns on his radio.'

'Are you taking requests on tonight's show?' I asked.

'You don't have to call in. I'll know what you need.'

At the next corner, she swung the Explorer right, onto Ocean Avenue. She drove uphill, away from the sea.

Fronting the shops and restaurants beyond the deep sidewalks, eighty-foot stone pines spread wings of branches across the street. The pavement was feathered with shadow and sunshine.

Moonlight Bay, home to twelve thousand people, rises from the harbor and flatlands into gentle serried hills. In most California travel guides, our town is called *The Jewel of the Central Coast*, partly because the chamber of commerce schemes relentlessly to have this sobriquet widely used.

The town has earned the name, however, for many reasons, not least of all because of our wealth of trees. Majestic oaks with hundred-year crowns. Pines, cedars, phoenix palms. Deep eucalyptus groves. My favorites are the clusters of lacy melaleucas luminaria draped with stoles of ermine blossoms in the spring.

As a result of our relationship, Sasha had applied protective film to the Explorer windows. Nevertheless, the view was shockingly brighter than that to which I was accustomed.

I slid my glasses down my nose and peered over the frames.

The pine needles stitched an elaborate dark embroidery on a wondrous purple-blue, late-afternoon sky bright with mystery, and a reflection of this pattern flickered across the windshield.

I quickly pushed my glasses back in place not merely to protect my eyes but because suddenly I was ashamed for taking such delight in this rare daytime journey even as my father lay dying.

Judiciously speeding, never braking to a full stop at those intersections without traffic, Sasha said, 'I'll go in with you.'

'That's not necessary.'

Sasha's intense dislike of doctors and nurses and all things medical bordered on a phobia. Most of the time she was convinced that she would live forever; she had great faith in the power of vitamins, minerals, antioxidants, positive thinking, and mind-body healing techniques. A visit to any hospital, however, temporarily shook her conviction that she would avoid the fate of all flesh.

'Really,' she said, 'I should be with you. I love your dad.'

Her outer calm was belied by a quiver in her voice, and I was touched by her willingness to go, just for me, where she most loathed to go.

I said, 'I want to be alone with him, this little time we have.'

'Truly?'

'Truly. Listen, I forgot to leave dinner out for Orson. Could you go back to the house and take care of that?'

'Yeah,' she said, relieved to have a task. 'Poor Orson. He and your dad were real buddies.'

'I swear he knows.'

'Sure. Animals know things.'

'Especially Orson.'

From Ocean Avenue, she turned left onto Pacific View. Mercy Hospital was two blocks away.

She said, 'He'll be okay.'

'He doesn't show it much, but he's already grieving in his way.'

'I'll give him lots of hugs and cuddles.'

'Dad was his link to the day.'

'I'll be his link now,' she promised.

'He can't live exclusively in the dark.'

'He's got me, and I'm never going anywhere.'

'Aren't you?' I asked.

'He'll be okay.'

We weren't really talking about the dog anymore.

The hospital is a three-story California Mediterranean structure built in another age when that term did not bring to mind uninspired tract-house architecture and cheap construction. The deeply set windows feature patinaed bronze frames. Ground-floor rooms are shaded by loggias with arches and limestone columns.

Some of the columns are entwined by the woody vines of ancient bougainvillea, which blankets the loggia roofs. This day, even with spring a couple of weeks away, cascades of crimson and radiant purple flowers overhung the eaves.

For a daring few seconds, I pulled my sunglasses down my nose and marveled at the sun-splashed celebration of color.

Sasha stopped at a side entrance.

As I freed myself from the safety harness, she put one hand on my arm and squeezed lightly. 'Call my cellular number when you want me to come back.'

'It'll be after sunset by the time I leave. I'll walk.'

'If that's what you want.'

'I do.'

Again I drew the glasses down my nose, this time to see Sasha Goodall as I had never seen her. In candlelight, her gray eyes are deep but clear – as they are here in the day world, too. Her thick mahogany hair, in candlelight, is as lustrous as wine in crystal – but markedly more lustrous under the stroking hand of the sun. Her creamy, rose-petal skin is flecked with faint freckles, the patterns of which I know as well as I know the constellations in every quadrant of the night sky, season by season.

With one finger, Sasha pushed my sunglasses back into place. 'Don't be foolish.'

I'm human. Foolish is what we *are*.

If I were to go blind, however, her face would be a sight to sustain me in the lasting blackness.

I leaned across the console and kissed her.

'You smell like coconut,' she said.

'I try.'

I kissed her again.

'You shouldn't be out in this any longer,' she said firmly.

The sun, half an hour above the sea, was orange and intense, a perpetual thermonuclear holocaust ninety-three million miles removed. In places, the Pacific was molten copper.

'Go, coconut boy. Away with you.'

Shrouded like the Elephant Man but for different reasons, I got out of the Explorer and hurried to the hospital, tucking my hands in the pockets of my leather jacket.

I glanced back once. Sasha was watching. She gave me a thumbs-up sign.

3

When I stepped into the hospital, Angela Ferryman was waiting in the corridor. She was a third-floor nurse on the evening shift, and she had come downstairs to greet me.

Angela was a sweet-tempered, pretty woman in her late forties: painfully thin and curiously pale-eyed, as though her dedication to nursing was so ferocious that, by the harsh terms of a devilish bargain, she must give the very substance of herself to ensure her patients' recoveries. Her wrists seemed too fragile for the work she did, and she moved so lightly and quickly that it was possible to believe that her bones were as hollow as those of birds.

She switched off the overhead fluorescent panels in the corridor ceiling. Then she hugged me.

When I had suffered the illnesses of childhood and adolescence – mumps, flu, chickenpox – but couldn't be safely treated outside of our house, Angela had been the visiting nurse who stopped in daily to check on me. Her fierce, bony hugs were as essential to the conduct of her work as were tongue depressors, thermometers, and syringes.

Nevertheless, this hug frightened more than comforted me, and I said, 'Is he?'

'It's all right, Chris. He's still holding on. Holding on just for you, I think.'

I went to the emergency stairs nearby. As the stairwell door eased shut behind me, I was aware of Angela switching on the ground-floor corridor lights once more.

The stairwell was not dangerously well lighted. Nevertheless, I climbed quickly and didn't remove my sunglasses.

At the head of the stairs, in the third-floor corridor, Seth

Cleveland was waiting. He is my father's doctor, and one of mine. Although tall with shoulders that seem round and massive enough to wedge in one of the hospital loggia arches, he manages never to be looming over you. He moves with the grace of a much smaller man, and his voice is that of a gentle fairy-tale bear.

'We're medicating him for pain,' Dr. Cleveland said, turning off the fluorescent panels overhead, 'so he's drifting in and out. But each time he comes around, he asks for you.'

Removing my glasses at last and tucking them in my shirt pocket, I hurried along the wide corridor, past rooms where patients with all manner of maladies, in all stages of illness, either lay insensate or sat before bed trays that held their dinners. Those who saw the corridor lights go off were aware of the reason, and they paused in their eating to stare at me as I passed their open doors.

In Moonlight Bay, I am a reluctant celebrity. Of the twelve thousand full-time residents and the nearly three thousand students at Ashdon College, a private liberal arts institution that sits on the highest land in town, I am perhaps the only one whose name is known to all. Because of my nocturnal life, however, not every one of my fellow townspeople has seen me.

As I moved along the hall, most of the nurses and nurses' aides spoke my name or reached out to touch me.

I think they felt close to me not because there was anything especially winning about my personality, not because they loved my father – as, indeed, everyone who knew him loved him – but because they were devoted healers and because I was the ultimate object of their heartfelt desire to nurture and make well. I have been in need of healing all of my life, but I am beyond their – or anyone's – power to cure.

My father was in a semiprivate room. At the moment no patient occupied the second bed.

I hesitated on the threshold. Then with a deep breath that did not fortify me, I went inside, closing the door behind me.

The slats of the Venetian blinds were tightly shut. At the periphery of each blind, the glossy white window casings glowed orange with the distilled sunlight of the day's last half hour.

On the bed nearest the entrance, my father was a shadowy shape. I heard his shallow breathing. When I spoke, he didn't answer.

He was monitored solely by an electrocardiograph. In order not to disturb him, the audio signal had been silenced; his heartbeat was traced only by a spiking green line of light on a cathode-ray tube.

His pulse was rapid and weak. As I watched, it went through a brief period of arrhythmia, alarming me, before stabilizing again.

In the lower of the two drawers in his nightstand were a butane lighter and a pair of three-inch-diameter bayberry candles in glass cups. The medical staff pretended to be unaware of the presence of these items.

I put the candles on the nightstand.

Because of my limitations, I am granted this dispensation from hospital rules. Otherwise, I would have to sit in utter darkness.

In violation of fire laws, I thumbed the lighter and touched the flame to one wick. Then to the other.

Perhaps my strange celebrity wins me license also. You cannot underestimate the power of celebrity in modern America.

In the flutter of soothing light, my father's face resolved out of the darkness. His eyes were closed. He was breathing through his open mouth.

At his direction, no heroic efforts were being taken to sustain his life. His breathing was not even assisted by an inhalator.

I took off my jacket and the Mystery Train cap, putting them on a chair provided for visitors.

Standing at his bed, on the side most distant from the candles, I took one of his hands in one of mine. His skin was cool, as thin as parchment. Bony hands. His fingernails were yellow, cracked, as they had never been before.

His name was Steven Snow, and he was a great man. He had never won a war, never made a law, never composed a symphony, never written a famous novel as in his youth he had hoped to do, but he was greater than any general, politician, composer, or prize-winning novelist who had ever lived.

He was great because he was kind. He was great because he was humble, gentle, full of laughter. He was married to my mother for thirty years, until her death two years previous to his, and during that long span of temptation, he had remained faithful to her. His love for her had been so luminous that our house, by necessity dimly lighted in most rooms, was bright in all of the ways that mattered. A professor of literature at Ashdon – where Mom had been a professor in the science department – Dad was so beloved by his students that many remained in touch with him decades after leaving his classroom.

Although my affliction had severely circumscribed his life virtually from the day that I was born, when he himself was twenty-eight, he had never once made me feel that he regretted fathering me or that I was anything less than an unmitigated joy and a source of undiluted pride to him. He lived with dignity and without complaint, and he never failed to celebrate what was *right* with the world.

Once he had been robust and handsome. Now his body was shrunken and his face was haggard, gray. He looked much older than his fifty-six years. The cancer had spread from his liver to his lymphatic system, then to other organs, until he was riddled with it. In the struggle to survive, he had lost much of his thick white hair.

On the cardiac monitor, the green line began to spike and trough erratically. I watched it with dread.

Dad's hand closed weakly on mine.

When I looked at him again, his sapphire-blue eyes were open and focused on me, as riveting as ever.

'Water?' I asked, because he was always thirsty lately, parched.

'No, I'm all right,' he replied, although he sounded dry. His voice was barely louder than a whisper.

I could think of nothing to say.

All of my life, our house was filled with conversation.

My dad and mom and I talked about novels, old movies, the follies of politicians, poetry, owls and deer mice and raccoons and bats and fiddler crabs and other creatures that shared the night with me, music, history, science, religion, art. Our discourse ranged from serious colloquies about the human condition to frothy gossip about neighbors. In the Snow family, no program of physical exercise, regardless of how strenuous, was considered to be adequate if it didn't include a daily workout of the tongue.

Yet now, when I most desperately needed to open my heart to my father, I was speechless.

He smiled as if he understood my plight and appreciated the irony of it.

Then his smile faded. His drawn and sallow face grew even more gaunt. He was worn so thin, in fact, that when a draft guttered the candle flames, his face appeared to be hardly more substantial than a reflection floating on the surface of a pond.

As the flickery light stabilized, I thought that Dad seemed to be in agony, but when he spoke, his voice revealed sorrow and regret rather than pain: 'I'm sorry, Chris. So damn sorry.'

'You've nothing to be sorry about,' I assured him, wondering if he was lucid or speaking through a haze of fever and drugs.

'Sorry about the inheritance, son.'

'I'll be okay. I can take care of myself.'

'Not money. There'll be enough of that,' he said, his whispery voice fading further. His words slipped from his pale lips almost as silently as the liquid of an egg from a cracked shell. 'The other inheritance . . . from your mother and me. The XP.'

'Dad, no. You couldn't have known.'

His eyes closed again. Words as thin and transparent as raw egg white: 'I'm so sorry . . .'

'You gave me *life*,' I said.

His hand had gone limp in mine.

For an instant I thought that he was dead. My heart fell stone-through-water in my chest.

But the beat traced in green light by the electrocardiograph showed that he had merely lost consciousness again.

'Dad, you gave me life,' I repeated, distraught that he couldn't hear me.

≈ ≈ ≈

My dad and mom had each unknowingly carried a recessive gene that appears in only one in two hundred thousand people. The odds against two such people meeting, falling in love, and having children are millions to one. Even then, both must pass the gene to their offspring for calamity to strike, and there is only one chance in four that they will do so.

With me, my folks hit the jackpot. I have xeroderma pigmentosum – XP for short – a rare and frequently fatal genetic disorder.

XP victims are acutely vulnerable to cancers of the skin and eyes. Even brief exposure to sun – indeed, to any ultraviolet rays, including those from incandescent and fluorescent lights – could be disastrous for me.

All human beings incur sunlight damage to the DNA – the genetic material – in their cells, inviting melanoma and other malignancies. Healthy people possess a natural repair system: enzymes that strip out the damaged segments of the neucleotide strands and replace them with undamaged DNA.

In those with XP, however, the enzymes don't function; the repair is not made. Ultraviolet-induced cancers develop easily, quickly – and metastasize unchecked.

The United States, with a population exceeding two hundred and seventy million, is home to more than eighty thousand dwarfs. Ninety thousand of our countrymen stand over seven feet tall. Our nation boasts four million millionaires, and ten thousand more will achieve that happy status during the current year. In any twelve months, perhaps a thousand of our citizens will be struck by lightning.

Fewer than a thousand Americans have XP, and fewer than a hundred are born with it each year.

The number is small in part because the affliction is so rare.

The size of this XP population is also limited by the fact that many of us do not live long.

Most physicians familiar with xeroderma pigmentosum would have expected me to die in childhood. Few would have bet that I could survive adolescence. None would have risked serious money on the proposition that I would still be thriving at twenty-eight.

A handful of XPers (my word for us) are older than me, a few significantly older, though most if not all of them have suffered progressive neurological problems associated with their disorder. Tremors of the head or the hands. Hearing loss. Slurred speech. Even mental impairment.

Except for my need to guard against the light, I am as normal and whole as anyone. I am not an albino. My eyes have color. My skin is pigmented. Although certainly I am far paler than a California beach boy, I'm not ghost white. In the candlelit rooms and the night world that I inhabit, I can even appear, curiously, to have a dusky complexion.

Every day that I remain in my current condition is a precious gift, and I believe that I use my time as well and as fully as it can be used. I relish life. I find delight where anyone would expect it – but also where few would think to look.

In 23 B.C., the poet Horace said, 'Seize the day, put no trust in the morrow!'

I seize the *night* and ride it as though it were a great black stallion.

Most of my friends say that I am the happiest person they know. Happiness was mine to choose or reject, and I embraced it.

Without my particular parents, however, I might not have been granted this choice. My mother and father radically altered their lives to shield me aggressively from damaging light, and until I was old enough to understand my predicament, they were required to be relentlessly, exhaustingly vigilant. Their selfless diligence contributed incalculably to my survival. Furthermore, they gave me the love – and the love of life – that made it impossible for me to choose depression, despair, and a reclusive existence.

My mother died suddenly. Although I know that she understood the profound depth of my feeling for her, I wish that I had been able to express it to her adequately on that last day of her life.

Sometimes, out in the night, on the dark beach, when the sky is clear and the vault of stars makes me feel simultaneously mortal and invincible, when the wind is still and even the sea is hushed as it breaks upon the shore, I tell my mother what she meant to me. But I don't know that she hears.

Now my father – still with me, if only tenuously – did not hear me when I said, 'You gave me life.' And I was afraid that he would take his leave before I could tell him all the things that I'd been given no last chance to tell my mother.

His hand remained cool and limp. I held it anyway, as if to anchor him to this world until I could say goodbye properly.

≈ ≈ ≈

At the edges of the Venetian blinds, the window frames and casings smouldered from orange to fiery red as the sun met the sea.

There is only one circumstance under which I will ever view a sunset directly. If I should develop cancer of the eyes, then before I succumb to it or go blind, I will one late afternoon go down to the sea and stand facing those distant Asian empires where I will never walk. On the brink of dusk, I'll remove my sunglasses and watch the dying of the light.

I'll have to squint. Bright light pains my eyes. Its effect is so total and swift that I can virtually feel the developing burn.

As the blood-red light at the periphery of the blinds deepened to purple, my father's hand tightened on mine.

I looked down, saw that his eyes were open, and tried to tell him all that was in my heart.

'I know,' he whispered.

When I was unable to stop saying what didn't need to be said, Dad found an unexpected reserve of strength and squeezed my hand so hard that I halted in my speech.

Into my shaky silence, he said, 'Remember . . .'

I could barely hear him. I leaned over the bed railing to put my left ear close to his lips.

Faintly, yet projecting a resolve that resonated with anger and defiance, he gave me his final words of guidance: 'Fear nothing, Chris. Fear nothing.'

Then he was gone. The luminous tracery on the electro-cardiogram skipped, skipped again, and went flatline.

The only moving lights were the candle flames, dancing on the black wicks.

I could not immediately let go of his slack hand. I kissed his forehead, his rough cheek.

No light any longer leaked past the edges of the blinds. The world had rotated into the darkness that welcomed me.

The door opened. Again, they had extinguished the nearest banks of fluorescent panels, and the only light in the corridor came from other rooms along its length.

Nearly as tall as the doorway, Dr. Cleveland entered the room and came gravely to the foot of the bed.

With sandpiper-quick steps, Angela Ferryman followed him, one sharp-knuckled fist held to her breast. Her shoulders were hunched, her posture defensive, as if her patient's death were a physical blow.

The ECG machine beside the bed was equipped with a telemetry device that sent Dad's heartbeat to a monitor at the nurses' station down the hall. They had known the moment that he slipped away.

They didn't come with syringes full of epinephrine or with a portable defibrillator to shock his heart back into action. As Dad had wanted, there would be no heroic measures.

Dr. Cleveland's features were not designed for solemn occasions. He resembled a beardless Santa Claus with merry eyes and plump rosy cheeks. He strove for a dour expression of grief and sympathy, but he managed only to look puzzled.

His feelings were evident, however, in his soft voice. 'Are you okay, Chris?'

'Hanging in there,' I said.

4

From the hospital room, I telephoned Sandy Kirk at Kirk's Funeral Home, with whom my father himself had made arrangements weeks ago. According to Dad's wishes, he was to be cremated.

Two orderlies, young men with chopped hair and feeble mustaches, arrived to move the body to a cold-holding room in the basement.

They asked if I wanted to wait down there with it until the mortician's van arrived. I said that I didn't.

This was not my father, only his body. My father had gone elsewhere.

I opted not to pull the sheet back for one last look at Dad's sallow face. This wasn't how I wanted to remember him.

The orderlies moved the body onto a gurney. They seemed awkward in the conduct of their business, at which they ought to have been practiced, and they glanced at me surreptitiously while they worked, as if they felt inexplicably guilty about what they were doing.

Maybe those who transport the dead never become entirely easy with their work. How reassuring it would be to believe as much, for such awkwardness might mean that people are not as indifferent to the fate of others as they sometimes seem to be.

More likely, these two were merely curious, sneaking glances at me. I am, after all, the only citizen of Moonlight Bay to have been featured in a major article in *Time* magazine.

And I am the one who lives by night and shrinks from the sight of the sun. Vampire! Ghoul! Filthy whacko pervert! Hide your children!

To be fair, the vast majority of people are understanding and kind. A poisonous minority, however, are rumor mongers who believe anything about me that they hear – and who embellish all gossip with the self-righteousness of spectators at a Salem witch trial.

If these two young men were of the latter type, they must have been disappointed to see that I looked remarkably normal. No grave-pale face. No blood-red eyes. No fangs. I wasn't even having a snack of spiders and worms. How boring of me.

The wheels on the gurney creaked as the orderlies departed with the body. Even after the door swung shut, I could hear the receding *squeak-squeak-squeak*.

Alone in the room, by candlelight, I took Dad's overnight bag from the narrow closet. It held only the clothes that he had been wearing when he'd checked into the hospital for the last time.

The top nightstand drawer contained his watch, his wallet, and four paperback books. I put them in the suitcase.

I pocketed the butane lighter but left the candles behind. I never wanted to smell bayberry again. The scent now had intolerable associations for me.

Because I gathered up Dad's few belongings with such efficiency, I felt that I was admirably in control of myself.

In fact, the loss of him had left me numb. Snuffing the candles by pinching the flames between thumb and forefinger, I didn't feel the heat or smell the charred wicks.

When I stepped into the corridor with the suitcase, a nurse switched off the overhead fluorescents once more. I walked directly to the stairs that I had climbed earlier.

Elevators were of no use to me because their ceiling lights couldn't be turned off independently of their lift mechanisms. During the brief ride down from the third floor, my sunscreen lotion would be sufficient protection; however, I wasn't prepared to risk getting stuck between floors for an extended period.

Without remembering to put on my sunglasses, I quickly descended the dimly lighted concrete stairs – and to my surprise, I didn't stop at the ground floor. Driven by a compulsion that I didn't immediately understand, moving faster than before, the suitcase thumping against my leg, I continued to the basement where they had taken my father.

The numbness in my heart became a chill. Spiraling outward from that icy throb, a series of shudders worked through me.

Abruptly I was overcome by the conviction that I'd relinquished my father's body without fulfilling some solemn duty, although I was not able to think what it was that I ought to have done.

My heart was pounding so hard that I could hear it – like the drumbeat of an approaching funeral cortege but in double time. My throat swelled half shut, and I could swallow my suddenly sour saliva only with effort.

At the bottom of the stairwell was a steel fire door under a red emergency-exit sign. In some confusion, I halted and hesitated with one hand on the push bar.

Then I remembered the obligation that I had almost failed to meet. Ever the romantic, Dad had wanted to be cremated with his favorite photograph of my mother, and he had charged me with making sure that it was sent with him to the mortuary.

The photo was in his wallet. The wallet was in the suitcase that I carried.

Impulsively I pushed open the door and stepped into a basement hallway. The concrete walls were painted glossy white. From silvery parabolic diffusers overhead, torrents of fluorescent light splashed the corridor.

I should have reeled backward across the threshold or, at least, searched for the light switch. Instead, I hurried recklessly forward, letting the heavy door sigh shut behind me, keeping my head down, counting on the sunscreen and my cap visor to protect my face.

I jammed my left hand into a jacket pocket. My right hand was clenched around the handle of the suitcase, exposed.

The amount of light bombarding me during a race along a hundred-foot corridor would not be sufficient, in itself, to trigger a raging skin cancer or tumors of the eyes. I was acutely aware, however, that the damage sustained by the DNA in my skin cells was cumulative because my body could not repair it. A measured minute of exposure each day for two months would have the same catastrophic effect as a one-hour burn sustained in a suicidal session of sun worship.

My parents had impressed upon me, from a young age, that the consequences of a single irresponsible act might appear negligible or even nonexistent but that inevitable horrors would ensue from *habitual* irresponsibility.

Even with my head tucked down and my cap visor blocking a direct view of the egg-crate fluorescent panels, I had to squint against the glare that ricocheted off the white walls. I should have put on my sunglasses, but I was only seconds from the end of the hallway.

The gray-and-red-marbled vinyl flooring looked like day-old raw meat. A mild dizziness overcame me, inspired by the vileness of the pattern in the tile and by the fearsome glare.

I passed storage and machinery rooms.

The basement appeared to be deserted.

The door at the farther end of the corridor became the door at the nearer end. I stepped into a small subterranean garage.

This was not the public parking lot, which lay above ground. Nearby were only a panel truck with the hospital name on the side and a paramedics' van.

More distant was a black Cadillac hearse from Kirk's Funeral Home. I was relieved that Sandy Kirk had not already collected the body and departed. I still had time to put the photo of my mother between Dad's folded hands.

Parked beside the gleaming hearse was a Ford van similar to the paramedics' vehicle except that it was not fitted with the standard emergency beacons. Both the hearse and the van were facing away from me, just inside the big roll-up door, which was open to the night.

Otherwise, the space was empty, so delivery trucks could pull inside to off-load food, linens, and medical supplies to the freight elevator. At the moment, no deliveries were being made.

The concrete walls were not painted here, and the fluorescent fixtures overhead were fewer and farther apart than in the corridor that I had just left. Nevertheless, this was still not a safe place for me, and I moved quickly toward the hearse and the white van.

The corner of the basement immediately to the left of the roll-up garage door and past those two waiting vehicles was occupied by a room that I knew well. It was the cold-holding chamber where the dead were kept until they could be transported to mortuaries.

One terrible January night two years ago, by candlelight, my father and I had waited miserably in cold holding more than half an hour with the body of my mother. We could not bear to leave her there alone.

Dad would have followed her from the hospital to the mortuary and into the crematorium furnace that night – if not for his inability to abandon me. A poet and a scientist, but such similar souls.

She had been brought from the scene of the accident by ambulance and rushed from the emergency room to surgery. She died three minutes after reaching the operating table, without regaining consciousness, even before the full extent of her injuries could be determined.

Now the insulated door to the cold-holding chamber stood open, and as I approached it, I heard men arguing inside. In spite of their anger, they kept their voices low; an emotional note of strenuous disagreement was matched by a tone of urgency and secrecy.

Their circumspection rather than their anger brought me to a stop just before I reached the doorway. In spite of the deadly fluorescent light, I stood for a moment in indecision.

From beyond the door came a voice I recognized. Sandy Kirk said, 'So who is this guy I'll be cremating?'

Another man said, 'Nobody. Just a vagrant.'

'You should have brought him to my place, not here,' Sandy complained. 'And what happens when he's missed?'

A third man spoke, and I recognized his voice as that of one of the two orderlies who had collected my father's body from the room upstairs: 'Can we for God's sake just move this along?'

Suddenly certain that it was dangerous to be encumbered, I set the suitcase against the wall, freeing both hands.

A man appeared in the doorway, but he didn't see me because he was backing across the threshold, pulling a gurney.

The hearse was eight feet away. Before I was spotted, I slipped to it, crouching by the rear door through which cadavers were loaded.

Peering around the fender, I could still see the entrance to the cold-holding chamber. The man backing out of that room was a stranger: late twenties, six feet, massively built, with a thick neck and a shaved head. He was wearing work shoes, blue jeans, a red-plaid flannel shirt – and one pearl earring.

After he drew the gurney completely across the threshold, he swung it around toward the hearse, ready to push instead of pull.

On the gurney was a corpse in an opaque, zippered vinyl bag. In the cold-holding chamber two years ago, my mother was transferred into a similar bag before being released to the mortician.

Following the stone-bald stranger into the garage, Sandy Kirk gripped the gurney with one hand. Blocking a wheel with his left foot, he asked again, 'What happens when he's missed?'

The bald man frowned and cocked his head. The pearl in his ear lobe was luminous. 'I told you, he was a vagrant. Everything he owned is in his backpack.'

'So?'

'He disappears – who's to notice or care?'

Sandy was thirty-two and so good-looking that even his grisly occupation gave no pause to the women who pursued him. Although he was charming and less self-consciously dignified than others in his profession, he made me uneasy. His handsome features seemed to be a mask behind which was not another face but an emptiness – not as though he were a different and less morally motivated man than he pretended to be, but as though he were no man at all.

Sandy said. 'What about his hospital records?'

'He didn't die here,' the bald man said. 'I picked him up earlier, out on the state highway. He was hitchhiking.'

I had never voiced my troubling perception of Sandy Kirk to anyone: not to my parents, not to Bobby Halloway, not to Sasha, not even to Orson. So many thoughtless people have made unkind assumptions about me, based on my appearance and my affinity for the night, that I am reluctant to join the club of cruelty and speak ill of anyone without ample reason.

Sandy's father, Frank, had been a fine and well-liked man, and Sandy had never done anything to indicate that he was less admirable than his dad. Until now.

To the man with the gurney, Sandy said, 'I'm taking a big risk.'

'You're untouchable.'

'I wonder.'

'Wonder on your own time,' said the bald man, and he rolled the gurney over Sandy's blocking foot.

Sandy cursed and scuttled out of the way, and the man with the gurney came directly toward me. The wheels squeaked – as had the wheels of the gurney on which they had taken away my father.

Still crouching, I slipped around the back of the hearse, between it and the white Ford van. A quick glance revealed that no company or institution name adorned the side of the van.

The squeaking gurney was rapidly drawing nearer.

Instinctively, I knew that I was in considerable jeopardy. I had caught them in some scheme that I didn't understand but that clearly involved illegalities. They would especially want to keep it secret from me of all people.

I dropped facedown on the floor and slid under the hearse, out of sight and also out of the fluorescent glare, into shadows as cool and smooth as silk. My hiding place was barely spacious enough to accommodate me, and when I hunched my back, it pressed against the drive train.

I was facing the rear of the vehicle. The gurney rolled past the hearse and continued to the van.

When I turned my head to the right, I saw the threshold of the cold-holding chamber only eight feet beyond the Cadillac. I had an even closer view of Sandy's highly polished black shoes and the cuffs of his navy-blue suit pants as he stood looking after the bald man with the gurney.

Behind Sandy, against the wall, was my father's small suitcase. There had been nowhere nearby to conceal it, and if I had kept it with me, I wouldn't have been able to move quickly enough or slip noiselessly under the hearse.

Apparently no one had noticed the suitcase yet. Maybe they would continue to overlook it.

The two orderlies – whom I could identify by their white shoes and white pants – rolled a second gurney out of the holding room. The wheels on this one did not squeak.

The first gurney reached the back of the white van. I heard the bald man open the rear cargo doors on that vehicle.

One of the orderlies said to the other, 'I better get upstairs before someone starts wondering what's taking me so long.' He walked away, toward the far end of the garage.

The collapsible legs on the first gurney folded up with a hard clatter as the bald man shoved it into the back of his van.

Sandy opened the rear door on the hearse as the remaining orderly arrived with the second gurney. On this one, evidently, was another opaque vinyl bag containing the body of the nameless vagrant.

A sense of unreality overcame me – that I should find myself in these strange circumstances. I could almost believe that I had somehow fallen into a dream without first falling into sleep.

The cargo-hold doors on the van slammed shut. Turning my head to the left, I watched the bald man's shoes as he approached the driver's door.

The orderly would wait here to close the big roll-up after the two vehicles departed. If I stayed under the hearse, I would be discovered when Sandy drove away.

I didn't know which of the two orderlies had remained behind, but it didn't matter. I was relatively confident that

I could get the better of either of the young men who had wheeled my father away from his death bed.

If Sandy Kirk glanced at his rear-view mirror as he drove out of the garage, however, he might see me. Then I would have to contend with both him and the orderly.

The engine of the van turned over.

As Sandy and the orderly shoved the gurney into the back of the hearse, I eeled out from under that vehicle. My cap was knocked off. I snatched it up and, without daring to glance toward the rear of the hearse, crabbed eight feet to the open door of the cold-holding chamber.

Inside this bleak room, I scrambled to my feet and hid behind the door, pressing my back to the concrete wall.

No one in the garage cried out in alarm. Evidently I had not been seen.

I realized that I was holding my breath. I let it out with a long hiss between clenched teeth.

My light-stung eyes were watering. I blotted them on the backs of my hands.

Two walls were occupied by over-and-under rows of stainless-steel morgue drawers in which the air was even colder than in the holding chamber itself, where the temperature was low enough to make me shiver. Two cushionless wooden chairs stood to one side. The flooring was white porcelain tile with tight grout joints for easy cleaning if a body bag sprang a leak.

Again, there were overhead fluorescent tubes, too many of them, and I tugged my Mystery Train cap far down on my brow. Surprisingly, the sunglasses in my shirt pocket had not been broken. I shielded my eyes.

A percentage of ultraviolet radiation penetrates even a highly rated sunscreen. I had sustained more exposure to hard light in the past hour than during the entire previous year. Like the hoofbeats of a fearsome black horse, the perils of cumulative exposure thundered through my mind.

From beyond the open door, the van's engine roared. The roar swiftly receded, fading to a grumble, and the grumble became a dying murmur.

The Cadillac hearse followed the van into the night. The

big motorized garage door rolled down and met the sill with a solid blow that echoed through the hospital's subterranean realms, and in its wake, the echo shook a trembling silence out of the concrete walls.

I tensed, balling my hands into fists.

Although he was surely still in the garage, the orderly made no sound. I imagined him, head cocked with curiosity, staring at my father's suitcase.

A minute ago I had been sure that I could overpower this man. Now my confidence ebbed. Physically, I was more than his equal – but he might possess a ruthlessness that I did not.

I didn't hear him approaching. He was on the other side of the open door, inches from me, and I became aware of him only because the rubber soles of his shoes squeaked on the porcelain tile when he crossed the threshold.

If he came all the way inside, a confrontation was inevitable. My nerves were coiled as tight as clockwork mainsprings.

After a disconcertingly long hesitation, the orderly switched off the lights. He pulled the door shut as he backed out of the room.

I heard him insert a key in the lock. The deadbolt snapped into place with a sound like the hammer of a heavy-caliber revolver driving the firing pin into an empty chamber.

I doubted that any corpses occupied the chilled morgue drawers. Mercy Hospital – in quiet Moonlight Bay – doesn't crank out the dead at the frenetic pace with which the big institutions process them in the violence-ridden cities.

Even if breathless sleepers were nestled in all these stainless-steel bunks, however, I wasn't nervous about being with them. I will one day be as dead as any resident of a graveyard – no doubt sooner than will other men of my age. The dead are merely the countrymen of my future.

I *did* dread the light, and now the perfect darkness of this cool windowless room was, to me, like quenching water to a man dying of thirst. For a minute or longer I relished the absolute blackness that bathed my skin, my eyes.

Reluctant to move, I remained beside the door, my back

against the wall. I half expected the orderly to return momentarily.

Finally I took off my sunglasses and slipped them into my shirt pocket again.

Although I stood in blackness, through my mind spun bright pinwheels of anxious speculation.

My father's body was in the white van. Bound for a destination that I could not guess. In the custody of people whose motivations were utterly incomprehensible to me.

I couldn't imagine any logical reason for this bizarre corpse swap – except that the cause of Dad's death must not have been as straightforward as cancer. Yet if my father's poor dead bones could somehow incriminate someone, why wouldn't the guilty party let Sandy Kirk's crematorium destroy the evidence?

Apparently they needed his body.

For what?

A cold dew had formed inside my clenched fists, and the back of my neck was damp.

The more I thought about the scene that I had witnessed in the garage, the less comfortable I felt in this lightless way station for the dead. These peculiar events stirred primitive fears so deep in my mind that I could not even discern their shape as they swam and circled in the murk.

A murdered hitchhiker evidently would be cremated in my father's place. But why kill a harmless vagrant for this purpose? Sandy could have filled the bronze memorial urn with ordinary wood ashes, and I would have been convinced that they were human. Besides, it was unlikely in the extreme that I would ever pry open the sealed urn once I received it – unlikelier still that I would submit the powdery contents for laboratory testing to determine their composition and true source.

My thoughts seemed tangled in a tightly woven mesh. I couldn't thrash loose.

Shakily, I withdrew the lighter from my pocket. I hesitated, listening for furtive sounds on the far side of the locked door, and then I struck a flame.

I would not have been surprised to see an alabaster corpse

silently risen from its steel sarcophagus, standing before me, face greasy with death and glimmering in the butane lambency, eyes wide but blind, mouth working to impart secrets but producing not even a whisper. No cadaver confronted me, but serpents of light and shadow slipped from the fluttering flame and purled across the steel panels, imparting an illusion of movement to the drawers, so that each receptacle appeared to be inching outward.

Turning to the door, I discovered that to prevent anyone from being accidentally locked in the cold-holding room, the deadbolt could be disengaged from within. On this side, no key was required; the lock could be operated with a simple thumbturn.

I eased the deadbolt out of the striker plate as quietly as possible. The doorknob creaked softly.

The silent garage was apparently deserted, but I remained alert. Someone could be concealed behind one of the supporting columns, the paramedics' van, or the panel truck.

Squinting against the dry rain of fluorescent light, I saw to my dismay that my father's suitcase was gone. The orderly must have taken it.

I did not want to cross the hospital basement to the stairs by which I had descended. The risk of encountering one or both of the orderlies was too great.

Until they opened the suitcase and examined the contents, they might not realize whose property it was. When they found my father's wallet with his ID, they would know I had been here, and they would be concerned about what, if anything, I might have heard and seen.

They had killed a hitchhiker not because he had known anything about their activities, not because he could incriminate them, but merely because they needed a body to cremate for reasons that still escaped me. With those who posed a genuine threat to them, they would be merciless.

I pressed the button that operated the wide roll-up. The motor hummed, the chain drive jerked taut overhead, and that big segmented door ascended with a frightful clatter. I glanced nervously around the garage, expecting to see an assailant break from cover and rush toward me.

When the door was more than halfway open, I stopped it with a second tap of the button and then brought it down again with a third. As it descended, I slipped under the door and into the night.

Tall pole lamps shed a brass-cold, muddy yellow light on the driveway that sloped up from the subterranean garage. At the top of the drive, the parking lot was also cast in this sullen radiance, which was like the frigid glow that might illuminate an anteroom to a precinct of Hell where punishment involved an eternity of ice rather than fire.

As much as possible, I moved through landscape zones, in the nightshade of camphor trees and pines.

I fled across the narrow street into a residential neighborhood of quaint Spanish bungalows. Into an alleyway without streetlamps. Past the backs of houses bright with windows. Beyond the windows were rooms where strange lives, full of infinite possibility and blissful ordinariness, were lived beyond my reach and almost beyond my comprehension.

Frequently, I feel weightless in the night, and this was one of those times. I ran as silently as the owl flies, gliding on shadows.

This sunless world had welcomed and nurtured me for twenty-eight years, had been always a place of peace and comfort to me. But now for the first time in my life, I was plagued by the feeling that some predatory creature was pursuing me through the darkness.

Resisting the urge to look over my shoulder, I picked up my pace and sprinted-raced-streaked-*flew* through the narrow back streets and darkways of Moonlight Bay.